"Detroit, *I See You Have* of company."

The Class Action: Division of Lawyers Monthly

"We are blowing our horn; number one for weeks and weeks, only Lottery tickets are out selling Ten Bridges……can't keep it on the shelf."

The Buckhorn Bugle (Dam Good Magazine)

"Brace yourself; if the auto industry makes this change, business will be down. We will have to wait patiently."

Billy Gamble, Actuary Consultant
Mortician's Table Monthly

"This book will definitely increase the price of recreational property on Rotten Lake."

Professor D Discern Ph.D. The Dummer Economist

"The Aggregate Truth is Out. Release your air brakes, sit back, relax and smoke your cigar. Cal is looking after us."

Warsaw Pit and Quarry Quarterly

"More than just money, well not so fast! We may have to change our marketing plans to fill those empty seats and load up the large collection plates."

Trust Us Monthly, The Preacher's Pulpit

"Evert and Rose have carefully slipped the steel ring off our finger and put it through our nose. I have tucked in my shirt tails so I don't lose that as well. They found a way to get even. We lost sight of what we were supposed to do. Well twisted, I am confused. Is this fiction or nonfiction? It sure is going to rewrite a few government specs. Fun to read if you are retired, I am out of here. To my colleagues, save our reputation, fix it quickly."

Wolfgang Herblinger Editor, Engineering:
The Rusty Steel Rings

"Carefully crafted country language captures the characters in an entertaining style reminiscent of a forgotten art. The story is larger than the economy of words and after the second read I reluctantly passed the book on to my best friend. Instead of my No Return policy I took the liberty of signing my name inside the front cover as I want it back."

Harvey Starkman, editor and critic for
The Readers' Society of South Asphodel

"Books are often written after the fact, but not this time."

Luella Loughton, Librarian, **Lakehurst Literary Lounge**

"There is now a shortage of back seats. Thanks to Ruthie, business is up in every parts bin."

Stew D. Baker Associate Editor:
Asphodel Auto Wreckers Press

"This Book will wipe new views."

        Truck and Auto Breaking News

"We will have to gear up for at least one tourist bus a year."

        The Norwood and Ouse River Tourist Bureau

Ten Bridges
Seven Churches
No Stop Light

Rodney Earl Andrews

Copyright © 2011 Rodney Earl Andrews
All rights reserved.

ISBN: 1461066735
ISBN-13: 9781461066736

Acknowledgements

Linda Butler read my very first rough cut and survived to read another day.

Daryl and Peter Neve gave me a few books to inspire and sound advice of their own.

Veronica and Yvan Gareau caught a number of typos and miss spells and said, "Publish the book!"

Jill and Dave Brett caught even more spelling errors, ouch again.

Amanda and Tom Mercer helped with the cover design, "You have to pick it up before you buy it."

Glen Sleeman the creative artist that covers the written word.

Lynda Pogue Kerr and Ray Kerr found the stories very interesting.

Heather Parker caught me repeating myself, in a senior's moment, on paper.

Annalee Mckechnie was the grunt editor who created sense out of chaos.

Lorraine Hill, final editor, who has done her best to make me look good.

Claire Archambault, my wife who listened to everything over and over, and is patiently listening to the second and third book!!!!

Michael Perrington, the video professional who captured the moment for all to see.

Dan Duran, the voice that caught your attention.

Norwood, "The Friendly Town" to all the characters who call it home.

A BIG THANKS TO YOU ALL

Rod

www.sawmillbooks.ca

About the Author

I am not a writer; I think I am a story teller.
I hope to be judged on keeping you
awake and entertained.

*I am like this little boy: He was playing in the mud
with a stick and writing on the sidewalk.
His mother comes along and asks him what he is doing.
He says, "I am writing."
"What does it say?"
"I don't know, I can't read, I can only write."*

Fiction is pure fiction
Good fiction is believable
Very good fiction... you are not sure if it's true
Excellent fiction... you will argue it's true
Outstanding fiction... it is the truth

Rod and Claire own and operate a Bed and
Breakfast on Pigeon Lake.
www.clairedelune.ca
Pigeon Lake is one of the Kawartha Lakes in
Ontario, Canada

This book is a work of fiction.
Names, places and characters are the product
of the author's imagination and experiences.

Places and names are used in a fictitious
manner. The stories were told and were they
true stories? We will never know as most of
the orators have left.

www.sawmillbooks.ca

Table of Contents

Chapter One	Jake Payne and The Fall Deer Hunt	1
Chapter Two	Sniper World War II	37
Chapter Three	Sometimes Teenagers Bump Into Love	47
Chapter Four	Ring The Bell, Stop The Line, Re-Tool	87
Chapter Five	The Brothers and the Bottle Trade	105
Chapter Six	Horses On Thin Ice	167
Chapter Seven	Walking Backwards You Stand Up Straighter	177

www.sawmillbooks.ca

CHAPTER ONE

Jake Payne and The Fall Deer Hunt

At one time in our history we were all hunters and gatherers and that is how we survived. Hunting was more than killing and the family fire was more than just for cooking. Step outside any major urban centre and you will still find everything stalls for the first two weeks in November as many skilled craftsmen we rely on are not answering their pagers. They are responding to a different calling. You do not have to pick up a bow or a rifle to join the Norwood men on the "Hunt." Hopefully this story will give you an insight into the ancient ritual.

North of Norwood, in Dummer Township, there are plenty of white-tailed deer. In some cases there are too many. The fall hunt is one way to keep their numbers in balance with their food supply. Dad and I were not hunters, but my brother and mother and many of my uncles enjoyed hunting. Some families are split that way. Some hunt and some choose not to.

I certainly enjoyed the many fine meals of game that my mother would cook. Partridge and rabbit were my favourites. This was all due to my brother's ability to shoot like a trained marksman. My brother loved to hunt, especially in the fall.

I was very proud that he never missed a partridge on the fly. His rifle, a .410 under and over, was short and easy to manoeuvre in the thickets. This rifle had a .22 barrel on top of the .410 shot gun barrel, and each chamber held one shot. I walked behind him and kept very quiet as we searched out hawthorn trees where partridges dined on fall berries. Ted was aware that we would be back to hunt next year, so he took only one or two birds per five acres. Ted would shoot a maximum of two on any walk in the woods, as that would be enough to feed mom, Ted, and me for lunch. If we did flush a partridge and it took flight, it was cleaned and in the bag within minutes. When we walked home from school at noon hour the three of us would have partridge stew, or if we were lucky, rabbit stew would be in the pot. Ted would watch out our kitchen window in the winter for rabbits eating raspberry canes. The loaded rifle in the corner of the kitchen would slowly stick out of the window and I, the non-hunter, would be in charge of going out to get the kill and completing the one last cleaning job before we were off to school.

The rabbit population had many predators, so good hunting occurred only one year out of seven. Fox and coyote populations respond to the food supply. Their numbers increase and decrease with the small game they can catch. If the fox population falls prey to rabies, rabbits multiply quickly.

Hunters, like Uncle Ken, ate everything they trapped. He said the best meal, the one he would have if it was his last, was roasted muskrat. I have not tasted muskrat, but some day I hope to have the opportunity.

Jake Payne

November first, the deer hunting season opened for a two-week period. Rifles and shotguns were both allowed in our area. Most hunters preferred using a rifle as it had a much longer range than a shotgun. Deer licences were issued by the provincial government along with a steel self-sealing tag to be inserted through the leg of the deer just above the hoof, as soon as the deer dropped. This is when a sharp knife came in handy. Many hunters put themselves in a jam with game wardens by not putting on their tags before bringing carcasses out of the woods to camp. Deer were plentiful and licences were issued - one per hunter and one for the camp kitchen.

Each November, Norwood District High School had a drop in the attendance of young male students, as a father's invitation to go to hunting camp was more attractive than the option of going to classes and doing homework. Teachers at the school knew students would be missing. Serious students would catch up when they got back. Yet, somehow, important tests and assignments were always scheduled around those first two weeks of November.

This would be Jake's second year in the hunting camp. Jake was fourteen. He purchased his first rifle when he turned twelve. Jake wanted a .22 calibre single shot rifle to go groundhog and rabbit hunting.

In those days, in the late-fifties, you never asked your parents to take you to town. You just hitch-hiked on Highway # 7 into Peterborough with or without a friend.

One spring Saturday morning Jake hitched a ride into Peterborough. This particular Saturday morning, he got a lift with Jack Warner, the owner of the fuel oil depot in Norwood. Jack drove a four or five-year-old Olds 98 and was going into Peterborough on business of some sort. The conversation got around to why Jake was going into town. Jack was pleased that his hitchhiker was a local boy, interested in getting rid of groundhogs, pesky creatures that created dangerous holes in which farm machinery broke axles and animals broke legs.

Jake was always amazed at the older men in town who could roll their own cigarettes. Jack Warner was an expert. On the stretch of highway going west, before the hill to Indian River, Jack pulled out to pass a truck, and at the same time, pulled out his tobacco pouch and papers. In the time it took him to put the tobacco on the paper, roll the cigarette, lick the glued edge, and strike the wooden match on the dash, he had passed the truck. This was all accomplished by steering with one hand and his left knee.

After that trip, Jake tried and perfected the ability to find a paper and fill it with tobacco and lick and light with one hand. He nicknamed his cigarettes "the Jack's." The pool hall crowd at Katie's was impressed the first time he performed the feat, and they soon copied this crowd-pleaser.

Getting dropped off on Lansdowne Street meant walking north on George Street to the Woolworth's Department Store. The store was located on the corner of Charlotte and George. The gun section was downstairs next to the budgie and other song birds' sales counter. Exactly eleven dollars and ninety-five cents was carefully counted out and the new .22 was his. No tax, since this was a few years before the so-called temporary federal and provincial sales taxes were introduced.

The middle-aged sales lady carefully put his new purchase into its cardboard gun case and thoughtfully brought to Jake's attention that he needed ammunition. Jake had forgotten about that but did have the money to purchase two boxes of bullets. There were fifty per box. He took his brother's advice and got longs, ammunition with a bit longer lead and more powder, so it would carry farther to the target. Later, his brother Harvey would show him how to drill a hole in the end of the lead to turn his longs into mushroom bullets to save an additional five cents per box.

Jake could hardly wait to get home. Walking south on George Street to Lansdowne seemed to take forever. When he reached the restaurant beside the Memorial Centre, he remembered that the extra money he had saved was intended for lunch. The restaurant on the southeast corner had the reputation of having the best fish and chips in town. They wrapped up your order in newspapers and it would stay warm until you got home. This would be a real surprise for his family. Today, there would be a treat to take home.

When Jake got home, his older brother admired the rifle and showed Jake how to use a rod to push string through the barrel and then, after removing the rod, how to pull the string and a wadded cloth full of oil slowly out of the barrel, removing all the little specks of lead and powder that were left in the spiral rifling. This procedure would have to be done two or three times until the barrel was perfectly clean. The rifling is the spiral etched into the inside wall of a barrel that turns the lead shot of the bullet into a twisting projectile. This keeps the shot more on target than if there is no rifling and the barrel has a smooth wall like that in a shotgun.

"Remember, Jake, always clean your .22 after you use it and then oil it. Keep it under your bed in this old towel, safe and sound. Don't leave bullets in it and leave the safety on." That was the end of that Hunter Safety Course. Jake had tailed his brother on so many hunts that he knew inside and out what to do and not to do with a rifle.

This year at hunting camp, Jake would use one of his Uncle Ross' deer rifles. His single shot .22 was not a suitable rifle for the deer hunt, as you wanted to be able to shoot a long straight distance and bring down your prize cleanly. He hoped to get his deer-hunting rifle on his sixteenth birthday - a lever action one like his grandfather's. It looked like the rifle that "The Rifleman" used on that television show. Jake was busy saving for something he really wanted and was prepared to wait another two years to acquire it. He knew that his parents could not afford to give him such an expensive gift for his sixteenth birthday. He also wanted to put notches on his own rifle.

Going to hunting camp was one of the major events of the year. In this camp, there were seven men, of which, Jake was the youngest. Seven men hunted, ate, played cards, drank, slept, and lived with each other for one or two weeks. Many years, it was three or four days, not two weeks. Once your limit was killed, camp broke for the year.

Deer have favourite paths or runs that they prefer to travel on and each person in the hunt camp would be assigned a run with an exact spot to wait for deer. At daylight you were on this run for at least two hours and, just before dark, you were on the same run for an hour. Deer are nocturnal, feeding at night and bedding down during the daylight hours. At dawn and dusk they are on the move. Deer can be persuaded to move faster if there is a trained dog running on their scent.

Hounds would be released in the morning on the main run. Their barking, sniffing, and howling would move the deer along the runways. You would get only one clean shot, if you were lucky, and the rule in this camp was that during the first week, you could shoot only at bucks, the male deer. Their horns would be easy to spot. Does were protected so they could have fawns the next spring, thus increasing the deer supply. In the years that deer were low in numbers, the buck rule was followed exclusively, and during the years of plenty, does did not have to be shot. Some camps in the area shot everything and even killed yearling fawns. This Norwood camp was a buck camp and these hunters looked down on other camps' traditions. Jake, being a teenager, thought it must be cool for the surviving bucks, which could have a harem.

The hunting camp was at the north end of Concession Eleven in Dummer Township and as far back in the cedar woods as a good half-ton truck could carry a full load. It was important to take a compass into the woods. To the north was a stretch of land over ten miles long with no roads and only man-made trails to find a way out. If you got lost, you might circle for a day or two, until a search party found you.

There was no electricity, no running water, no phone, but there was a two-seater outhouse. Modern times had come and the catalogue from Eaton's or Sears was no longer hung on a hanger. Instead, modern toilet paper, carefully placed in a waterproof, mouse-proof can, was always available to do the job. Shiny catalogue paper was not missed. It did, however, provide reading material when time to wait was required.

Water had to be trucked in and old cream cans with their tight-fitting lids worked well. Groceries and necessities were trucked in on the first day, as few men wanted to leave camp to go to town or home to get something they had forgotten. The Camp List grew longer every year, and soon it took more that one truckload to bring everything into camp. Wood, cigar, pipe, and cigarette smoke filled the camp, because in the fifties, just about everyone smoked or chewed something. One tradition, that remains today, is that the mattresses were filled with fresh straw each year. It was one person's responsibility to get fresh straw and fill each mattress cover. Old timers loved the smell and the texture of their beds. It brought back memories of the days when they would be sent off to the woods to cut firewood for the winter. Straw mattresses were used only for the hunt and, at the break-up of camp; they were emptied outside to make a pile of bedding for deer or a home for all sorts of small animals and rodents.

Leaving the straw inside invited mice to take up residence and make a mess that had to be cleaned the following year.

The duties of all seven men in the hunt camp were sorted out in advance each year. No one needed to be reminded or told twice what his responsibilities were. Jake, being the youngest and the most recent member, was in charge of firewood and garbage. Each year, firewood would be cut, split, and piled so it was dry for the next season. Small limbs of wood and finely-split hardwood were piled for the cook stove and larger chunks were piled separately for the box stove that heated the balance of the camp. These two stoves would use almost two cords of wood if the hunt lasted a week, and double if they needed the second week. If it turned cold and snowy, you burned more. During the day, when Jake was not hunting, he was busy cutting and gathering wood for next year. Most men would rather be out working than sitting around, so Jake did not have to do all the work by himself. A couple of short days, and cut wood was brought back to camp. Then Jake could build his muscles splitting and piling.

Garbage detail was easy, as garbage was wrapped and burned in the box stove along with the wood. Only cans and glass jars were bagged and taken out of camp. Leaving any garbage around invited black bears to break into camp and rummage around for a snack. Bears would not come near the camp during hunting season as most camps had bear licences and bears would be shot. Bear meat is very tasty and any game, including the venison, was divided among the hunters at the end of camp. Ron, one of the camp crew, hunted game all year and had a trapping licence. Extra bear meat would help fill his family's freezer. He would not allow his family to eat any store-bought meat as he said he did not trust what was in the meat. He knew wild game was good and he wanted his family to eat healthy.

The hunt camp was a good size, twenty feet by twenty-four feet, with a kitchen and dining room table at one end and four sets of bunks and a double bed at the other end of the large open room. The kitchen sink's grey water ran out into a forty-gallon steel drum that was buried in a hole with a lot of gravel around it for suitable drainage. Grey water included all used water, except for the flushing water from a toilet.

Extra beds were for visitors who dropped in during the hunt. As the evening wore on, somehow some hunters could not find their legs to go home and there was no need for someone to take them home. Jake's dad would hide their truck keys and the men never could find them, even if they wanted to go home. Men looked after each other, in camp and out.

One tradition Jake found interesting was that all the chairs were hung on the wall after the meal and were taken down only if the men wanted to play cards or sit around the stove in the candlelight, when all the catch-up stories would be spun out for the fun of the evening. Hanging the chairs up on the wall created more space and it also made it very easy to sweep the floor and to clean up.

This was a typical camp. During the day, the men did not want to be inside and found ways to busy themselves out and about. Manley, a finishing carpenter, always had something to keep every idle hand busy. One year they might put on eaves troughs; another year they might install new windows, build cupboards, or attach a lean-to for extra wood storage. Over the years, the main camp building was improved and the modern conveniences of home would show up. Having a carpenter and a smattering of all the house-building trades among the camp members brought rich rewards.

The roof of the camp was made from spruce and tamarack poles sheeted with one-by-six boards and covered with layers of tar paper. This made it watertight but not heat tight. The walls were very much the same. On a cold day most people stayed in the center of the building. Jake kept the fires burning and would wake up in the middle of the night to load more wood into the stoves. Jake was just fourteen. This would be his second and last year hunting at the camp.

Jake's elementary school was a one-room brick schoolhouse within easy walking distance of his family's farm. In grade five, at eleven years of age, he was given the job of starting the school wood stove and cleaning out the ashes during the heating season. The heating season lasted from late October until the beginning of May. His part time job paid twenty-five cents a week and would provide Jake with his pocket money and savings to buy the things he really wanted, like the .22 calibre single shot rifle.

The job bore a huge responsibility as Jake had to arrive at school ahead of the teacher and students and make sure the room was warm for the nine o'clock morning start. He walked to school, cleaned out the ashes, started a fire, and, as it was heating, he would pound the blackboard erasers against the outside brick wall to get them clean for the day. All the pencils left in the box the previous day were sharpened, as no one was allowed to sharpen pencils once class started. With students in seven of the eight grades, the teacher was busy, and did not need someone grinding pencils when she was explaining the day's lessons.

For average and bright students, the one-room school, with a capable teacher was the best place for a young mind to be. In grade four you would get to hear the grade two and three students receive their lessons and you could also listen in and follow the grade five and six students. Reinforcement and practice made a recipe for success. Bright students like Jake would read when they were finished their work. They also were assigned younger brothers, sisters or neighbour kids in the junior grades. The older helpers, now called tutors, were in charge of marking papers, correcting errors, and keeping their charges up to date on their studies. Idle time was spent reading. Most students had read every book in the school's two-drawer library and could hardly wait for magazines, newspapers, and any print material Miss Small would bring to school.

One day, Jake overhead his dad talking to a local school trustee. Jake had been hired to replace a student who had just graduated from grade eight. The trustee said, "The woodshed is full of good dry hardwood, and it is more than enough to last one winter. We have never burned a complete shed of wood, even in the coldest of winters." Jake promptly took up the challenge. Purposefully, he arrived early every morning and put into place a system of quickly removing cold ashes and starting a new fire with kindling. He added extra kindling and propped the damper open to allow more air into the fire box. He started with a bed of cedar and poplar, and then gradually switched to maple and beech. Ironwood was saved for really cold days.

When the teacher arrived at seven forty-five sharp every day, the school was toasty and smelled like a new fresh day. Miss Small was full of smiles and praise, and sometimes a small treat was placed on Jake's desk. This was the first time she could remember arriving at a school and being able to take off her gloves and coat to start her board work for the day.

Jake always put the box of chalk carefully next to the stove to warm it. The sawdust that chalk was packed in was prized. This tinder-dry sawdust would be used for a quick start on a freezing cold day when a faster fire was needed.

Blackboards were made of real slate. One day, while waiting for Miss Small to arrive, having read everything there was to read in the school, Jake found a note tucked away in the bottom of the chalk brush box.

CARE OF SLATE

Friday

Brush off all the chalk dust and clear chalk rails.
Soak a soft rag with warm water and rub it generously into a Sunlight soap bar.
Soap the slate, do all six slates.
Start with the first and wipe off before the slates are dry.

Jake's mom would not miss small pieces of Sunlight bar soap. Jake was curious to see if the instructions on the note worked. At the end of the next school day, Jake took longer than usual to bring in some firewood. He was hoping the school would clear, so he could try Sunlight soap on a side slate board. Each week the boards got blacker and blacker and easier to write on. The school inspector even praised Miss Small on how she maintained all the boards in the school. Jake's mom was happy to supply a new big bar of Sunlight. One Friday, after everyone had left for the weekend, Jake was in the process of soaping the slates, when the door flew open, and in came Miss Small to pick up a stack of marking that she had left behind. She took one look at Jake and the boards and said nothing. Jake was sure she winked.

Needless to say, in the spring, the school trustee could not believe that the wood shed was completely empty. Jake was hired to fill the shed for the next fall. When Jake moved on to high school at the end of grade eight, the school trustee decided it was time to put in an oil furnace. No other student would have the responsibility and fun that Jake had enjoyed for four years.

With all this practice, keeping the hunting camp warm would be a piece of cake for Jake. He soon had everyone sitting in their undershirts.

Hunting camps are passed down from generation to generation and many a man wished that his long life would end at camp. A neighbour, Mr Payne, no close relation to Jake, died on the hunt under the arms of a large maple tree while on morning watch. This was the way to go, doing the things you loved to do. Mr. Payne's death made room for Jake at the hunt camp.

Father, son, brother, uncle, neighbours, and friends, all men with a common interest in hunting deer, made up most of the camps around the Norwood area. Each camp and hunting area supported a limited number of hunters. Openings came up only when people moved away from the area or when age, disease or illness overtook someone. Fathers always had the first opportunity to invite their sons. If there were no sons, other names would be discussed and a consensus would be reached about who would be invited for the next year. Jake's dad was a wise master at inviting new members, as good chemistry among the group made for a more enjoyable hunt. The temporary tribe replaced the outside world and the yearly draw to the camp bound men together.

In his second year at camp, Jake was expected to take over some of the kitchen duties, and he quickly volunteered to make the morning snack for the men to take out with them with their coffee on the first hunt of the day. Jake's favourite breakfast snack was a fried-egg sandwich. A little bacon, two eggs with the yolk broken, over-easy twice, put between two pieces of homemade bread, toasted with a little splatter of mayonnaise, and wrapped in waxed paper. This was a welcome treat out on the deer run.

On the first day of the hunt that year, three bucks were shot. One large and two averaged-size deer were hung from the large oak tree by the camp. Deer were bled, gutted, and then hung in a tree or from a large post stand until the hunt was over. A stand is like the gate opening that you expect to see at the entrance to a cattle ranch. The main difference is that the upright posts on a deer stand are supported on all four sides, so the weight of a carcass will not tip the stand. The stand was always placed close to camp and a rifle shot would discourage any poacher - human or animal. A carcass was hung with the head and hide still on. Hanging the deer served a number of purposes. Bears, coyotes, and other animals could not make off with the catch or chew away at it. More importantly, the meat had a chance to start aging so it would be more tender and easier to prepare.

In Norwood a number of families would come home from the hunt to hang deer carcasses on a tree in the front yard or on the eave of a tall shed. Rusaws, La Brashes, and the Shoups always had the largest line of hanging game. One year, in the big elm on the La Brashes' front lawn, hung a bull moose. It made deer carcasses look tiny.

Highway # 7 was filled with cars heading back to the city with deer on their front and back fenders. Half-ton trucks were not as common in the sixties as they are today. Anyone with the luxury of time to sit and watch, would have counted over one hundred deer per hour going from hunt camps back to the city. This traffic would continue for a week to ten days from morning to night. People who watched this parade were often envious, wishing they themselves had been fortunate enough to have such success in the hunt.

BACK TO THE NORWOOD CAMP.

On the second day of the hunt, it rained and rained and the dogs were not able to rouse anything. The third day would be perfect. Overnight, a cold north wind dried up the ground and a dusting of snow painted the landscape completely white. The sun was out and the temperature down, and with no wind, snow stayed on the trees, shrubs, and tall grass. Short hawthorn trees, dusted in white, gave a glimpse of what hot African plains might look like if it ever snowed there. This would be a good day and the camp quota would probably be filled, so it could mean one more night in camp, ending a short year, as the deer in this neck of the woods were plentiful once again.

Each man was assigned a run. Every hunter knew how to get to his run and how to return to camp safely. Rifle shots carry a long way and no one wants to be in the wrong place at the wrong time. Hunting camps, even if they were right beside each other, were safe because experienced hunters never crossed their own camp's boundaries. When trailing a wounded deer or bear, you stopped at your camp line. If a wounded animal came into your area, it was yours to shoot. An unwritten rule, when any animal crossed camp lines, was to split the meat with the camp that started the kill. That was the only time a doe or fawn would be shot in this camp.

The first year Jake was part of the hunt, his dad, Clint went over and over with Jake all the runs and boundaries pointing out where everyone would be. There had never been a mistake in the past. They all hoped there would be none in the future. Jake knew their camp area well, as he had been in these woods since age eight helping the family cut and split firewood for the year. Feeding his parents' kitchen wood stove and wood furnace, plus doing the same for his grandparents, meant that every spare Saturday afternoon was spent in the woods.

Wednesday morning, everyone dressed warmly, packed a fried egg sandwich in a coat pocket and headed out to his assigned run. Jerry was in charge of the dogs. He would wait until he was sure everyone was in place, and then he would release them.

Jake filled up the wood stove with three large blocks of sugar maple wood, topped up the side water reservoir, and put enough beech wood into the wood box stove to hold the fire until he returned. He knew that the cabin would be warm and the cook stove ready for cooking breakfast. He would add six or seven small pieces of maple, and the frying pans would be hot and ready to cook.

Jake stepped out of the camp door with both of his sandwiches. Being the cook and having a young hollow leg to fill, there would be lots of room for two sandwiches. Jake realized he was not dressed warmly enough. He went back in, took off his overalls, and put on his fleece-lined pullover, his high school sweater. Jake had just purchased a NDHS sweater at school a couple of months beforehand during "September Spirit Week." He was sure that it would be thick enough to keep him warm on the run.

Jake's run was the farthest away from camp as young legs were given the longest distance to travel. The night's dusting of snow showed every track, like those of rabbits bouncing from place to place. Fox tracks were the most interesting. You could follow these tracks to the end before realizing that the sly fox had doubled back moving left or right with a large jump. A weasel track with its sprocket-like appearance went across Jake's trail. The prints most hunters did not want to see were a wolf's or coyote's. These populations were increasing and many deer hunters would give up a shot at a deer if a coyote was present. The rule for coyotes was SSS: shoot, shovel, and shut up. Beef farmers were losing young calves to smart and nimble coyotes and dead beef represented lost income. Cows have one calf a year, unless they have twins, so a cow's yearly production could disappear in one meal for coyotes. The quickest way to reduce the coyote population was to watch for a cow ready to calve and scoop up the afterbirth with a shovel before the other cows or farm dogs could eat it. Farmers took the afterbirth, placed it near the edge of the woods and waited to the left or right of a downwind for the coyotes.

Jake was anxious to bag his second deer and make it two years in a row. Last year for his first hunt, Jake was partnered with his Uncle Ken. This was standard procedure in training new hunters, teaching them the rules and procedures of working, hunting, and having fun at camp. Uncle Ken told Jake about an old buck that had been sighted for a number of years but never shot. Each year a buck grows more points on the rack, and as it gets older, each new rack gets another point. Many hunters count the points, which they believe gives the age of the buck. To survive, a buck has to be wise and skittish and avoid being shot or eaten. This old buck, that everyone talked about, would have a record rack for magazines to write about.

Jake, at thirteen, and his Uncle Ken were on their run when the buck appeared. They looked in wonder as this thin old deer stared back at them. Growing out of its head appeared to be a full-grown staghorn sumac tree. Before Jake could take aim, the buck bounded over the hill and was gone. Jake, not knowing that you can never catch a deer, made a snap decision to run after the buck up the rise to see where it had gone. Uncle Ken could not keep up to the young lad and followed behind. At the top of the hill he saw Jake lift his rifle. He heard a shot. The buck had stopped and looked back, as Jake broke over the hill. This fine old buck stayed in perfect formation for a clean shot.

Its head was very old and had a record-breaking rack. The carcass, though, dressed out with less meat than a year-old doe, as the animal was probably in its last year of life. The meat was turned into sausage. Everyone knew that you could not chew that old buck.

A number of hunting magazines picked up the story. Jake, in his first year at camp, had that trophy rack many hunters waited for all their lives. Having the head mounted was an option, but it would be expensive and the head was looking old. Saving just the rack was the best thing in this case. What do you do to follow that record?

Jake, although only fourteen, knew that his success last year had no bearing on this year's hunt. He was just hoping to get a shot at a buck, and be able to tell the story back in camp. Jake walked to his run and brushed off the snow on an old oak stump. He put a couple of cedar branches under his butt to keep the cold from penetrating. He was prepared to sit there motionless for two hours, waiting, listening, and hoping a buck would head down his run. He heard dogs barking, but they were off his trail, and he could only imagine his dad on the west run getting a good shot. A few moments later he heard a shot that came from his dad's run, and given the single shot fired, it was either a clean kill or a miss.

Time crawled by and all he could hear were dogs in the distance. It seemed that the deer had decided to go north in the direction of the night's wind and not to move south. Clearly, the hunt would not end today as one kill would not fill their licence quota. It was time to eat the second sandwich and be patient.

After two hours of waiting, he decided to walk back to camp. He had fun thinking about what would be served for breakfast today. A small breeze had picked up, and snow had started to drift off the branches of the maples, oaks, and elms. The sun caught the crystals. It was quiet and very peaceful. The snow on the ground took the crunch of leaves and twigs out of Jake's step. The sun started to climb, making it hot. Jake realized that the extra sweat shirt was just too much clothing. His NDHS sweat top was white with blue and gold lettering. He opened the front of his overalls to cool down. Jake did not realize that the front of his overalls formed a perfect white V-shape. All would have been well, but just as he was getting close to camp, he saw two coyotes slink off to one side of the hill. SSS, shoot, shovel, and shut-up, was the rule and he decided to move over a bit to the east to take a shot and drop one of the predators.

Meanwhile, just over the rise, Manley spotted a buck drifting north. He had his gun up with its sight aimed just below the rack. He saw the buck turn and flash its white tail. He was sure it would be a clean shot. He controlled his breath and slowly pulled the trigger.

The bullet hole entered just above the crossbar in the H of NDHS. Jake never felt a thing, falling backwards, as a lead mushroom bullet drilled through his heart and tore out his back.

Manley was in shock when he walked over to the kill site. No buck, just Jake lying on his back. Manley, a sniper in the

Second World War, had made a practice of never looking at his completed work. This was the first time he had killed a human and seen the result.

The word of Jake's death spread through the hunting camps. Hunters from miles around decided that they should pay their respects and attend the funeral. Not everyone knew Jake and his family, but everyone had met or heard of Reeve Manley. Every hunter who picks up a rifle or a bow fears the day that he will pull the trigger and not hit the target that he expects.

The hunt was over for this year.

THE FUNERAL

SATURDAY, NOVEMBER 7TH, 1960.

News of the tragedy spread quickly through town and all the hunting camps. High school students were informed by an announcement on the PA system at 3:14 p.m., one minute before the end of the last class. Jake's older brother, Harvey, had been part of last year's hunt, but decided not to go this year, as he needed every last mark on June's departmental exams, so he could go to university. The vice-principal took Harvey and Rose aside and tried to tell them the news without breaking down. He wanted the brother and sister to hear the news before the principal made the PA announcement to the student body. Everyone was in shock. No one wanted to believe the news.

On the southeast corner on the main street in Norwood stood a hydro pole bristling with tacks and staples. This was where death cards were posted for public viewing. The *Norwood Register* was the town's only paper and it published weekly. It told you what had happened and what was going to happen, but it could not deliver immediate news. That news was posted on the hydro pole. Obituaries were found in the back section of the *Peterborough Examiner* and that is why that paper was read back to front by subscribers who would say, "Good. My name is not there. Now, who has died and what is going on?"

In Norwood, the church and the funeral home were both possible places to hold the service. Jake's body would be embalmed and the three-day mourning period would begin. The question was where would the final service be held? At that time, the United Church, like many Protestant churches was trying to cut costs. Realizing that funerals added costs not revenues, churches hoped to get funeral homes to pick up the cost of a service. The minister would gladly go to the funeral home to conduct the service as this did not require heating up the church and cleaning after people had left. Churches were only interested in providing a paid luncheon in the basement after the graveyard service. The funeral home, a business-for-profit, saw the opportunity to provide the complete service, justifying a hefty fee.

The funeral director and the minister, a new recruit after the retirement of Reverend Wright, realized that Jake's funeral was going to be too large for the funeral home to conduct. A church would have to provide the service. Then, a form would be filled out to explain to the authorities in the head office why the funeral was held in church. The United Church Minister was expecting one to two-hundred people to attend the funeral, which, he estimated would require four or five hours of extra caretaking time and added expenses for cleanup after the casket was gone.

However, over one thousand people attended and the church, front steps, and lawn were filled with mourners and spectators. The procession to the graveyard was a continuous line of cars and trucks stretching from the church to the gravesite.

The traditional pallbearers were cousins and friends of Jake's. Many students from NDHS attended, as well as all the kids who had gone to elementary school with Jake. This community tragedy touched the heart of a wide range of people in and around Norwood.

The United Church Minister was new to town, new to the ministry, and was grasping to find a meaningful sermon. He took out a funeral eulogy template provided by head office and was busy talking to friends and relatives to find key words to fill in the blanks, so the sermon would sound as if he knew Jake, the family, and the town's feelings. The Reverend also realized that this was an opportunity to establish his reputation, not only with the church members but also with the community at large. He worked hard. This is where a good partner comes in. His wife watched her husband working and suggested, "Why not call the retired Reverend Wright to help conduct the service?" Reverend Wright was very pleased to get the call and he led the proceedings and coached the new minister on how this funeral should flow.

Norwood cemetery, mainly full of Protestants, is on the north side of the esker that divides the town in two. In November the ground has not frozen and a site can be strobed and dug, so the body does not have to go into the crypt to wait for a spring burial. The men who dig graves always push a thin metal pole or strobe into the ground to find out what is below.

At the grave site, the front row was given to Jake's parents and the other five members of the hunting camp. Manley stood in the center of the group. As the casket was lowered into the grave, the minister drew a white sand cross onto the head of the casket with his aluminum push-button cylinder. The creaking of the straps while the casket was lowered, reminded all that their turn would come sometime in the future.

What most mourners did not notice was Jake's twin sister, Rose moving over beside Manley and quietly slipping her hand into his. her hand into his. Rose worshiped her older brother, older by a mere fifteen minutes. Everyone in and outside the family expected sisters and brothers not to get along, but Jake and Rose had a special relationship. They did everything together. They took on their small world as a formidable team. They had a pact.

The casket was being lowered and reality set in.

When people attend a funeral they do four things. One, they look around at all the headstones and realize that they are in a cemetery; two, they read names to see if they recognize someone buried there; three, they realize that some day they will be here or in another cemetery; and four, they think about why they are here today.

Jake's family touched many people in Norwood and now, as they stood at the gravesite, they all thought about this family. Reverend Wright had a special talent in reaching one's soul. During the service, after the Thirty-Second Psalm was read, the Reverend paused. He raised his voice and looked at the crowd in a three-hundred-and-sixty-degree circle. He said, "I served in the Second World War and Remembrance Day is soon approaching. I have found the minute of silence to be the most important part of my life. I want you to take two minutes now to think of the best time, the most important time, the toughest time, the time you should have spent with Jake. We will be silent. I don't want you to close your eyes, as I invite you to look over at that hill to the south and see Jake and his twin sister Rose screaming with laughter and filling their faces with snow as they careen out of control down the hill."

While growing up, Rose often thought about how poorly Jake dressed. Jake would put on clothes only because he had to wear them. The hat was on his head, his shirt was buttoned up, and his pants were on. Colours matching or clothes fitting were not his concerns. The best way to think of Jake was - yes, the hat is on. Rose and other young girls saw Jake's potential and thought if only they could get their hands on him to make improvements. Jake was too busy talking, listening, and teasing to worry about what he looked like. If he was warm in the winter and cool in the summer, he had spent enough time on that chore. Jake's best day was when he had to dress only once. To change clothes more than once was an absolute punishment. Skinny-dipping in the local creek was the ultimate freedom.

Hank, Jake's best friend, who lived on the farm next over, sat either behind him or in front of him in every grade of elementary school. Each grade had its row in the one-room school. Where you sat depended on who was growing the fastest and who was the tallest. The shortest student sat at the front and the tallest one sat at the back. It seemed each year, Jake and Hank would trade places with each other. The year they graduated to Norwood District High School, all students were streamed. Students with the highest marks were in 9A and those with the lowest marks were in 9E. Again, Hank and Jake ended up in the same class. They rode the same bus together and ate lunch side-by-side in the cafeteria. Hank was busily trying to fit in and envied Jake, who was a roller, having fun with the new experience of high school, meeting kids from Hastings, Havelock, Norwood, Cordova, and Centre Dummer.

Once a month, there was a sock hop in the school gymnasium on the last Friday of the month. Friday buses would be held back and would not take students home until 9:00 o'clock. Jake loved to dance and he always seemed to be on the floor. Girls would sit on steel chairs against the south wall, and guys would sit on steel chairs on the north wall.

Once a record started, each guy would figure out if he could move to the music, and if he could, and had the courage, he would walk across the gym and ask the girl he had been admiring for a dance. Jake was on the floor all the time. The girls wanted to dance, not to sit, and they would dance with anyone once or twice just to get up. Jake discovered this secret early and worked his way down the line. Jake was there to dance and all the girls could hardly wait to be asked.

At the gravesite, Brenda broke out in uncontrolled laughter. To Brenda it seemed to last forever, but for the quiet crowd, it was short. Some people in tragic situations are so overwrought, that instead of crying, the socially-acceptable behaviour, they break out laughing.

Brenda was the hockey coach's daughter, who attended every game her dad coached. During practices she would put on her skates, boys' skates, not figure skates with points on the front. Brenda would always correct her hockey guys and she would say, "They are picks not points. Do you want to pick a fight or get poked?" Jake would always find a way to set her up, so she could score a goal. The coach's daughter was off limits for a rough stick-check, or a push into the boards or goal post. Brenda made practices fun as players could see she was trying as hard as they were and having as much fun.

The coach had two older sons who were grown up and long gone when along came a surprise, Brenda. He forgot most of the times that his daughter was a girl and took her places, just like he had done with his two sons. If he needed a spare goalie, she would put the pads; if he needed a forward, or a defenseman, she would fill that role. Brenda was also secretly in love with Jake and would make sure she was in the dance line at sock hops.

Jean was just one of the many high school students who crowded the cemetery that day. Jean had been in the same grade as Jake all through elementary school and was in Jake's home form in grade nine. English class, first thing in the morning, all year long. One September, Jean did not feel well, and by the middle of October was in Princess Margaret Hospital in Toronto losing her hair to a cancer treatment.

Jean always watched Jake from afar. Shy, with only sisters, how do you act around boys especially the ones you like?

Jean returned to school in late November with no hair. The only wig her parents could afford looked like a wig. She dreaded going back but she knew she must. Getting on a cold school bus on Monday morning, she carefully pulled down a toque to hide that wig.

Sitting in her designated bus seat just behind Jake, she rode that lonely trip to school. After getting off the bus, walking down the hall, opening up her locker, and taking off her winter coat, Jean slipped into the girls' washroom to remove her toque and comb her artificial hair.

The bell rang and everyone was seated. Jean felt all eyes were on her. Then the laughing started and she could not bear it, until she looked up and there was Jake with his head completely shaved. The teacher, who was naturally bald, did not miss a beat and said, "Welcome back, Jean. Jake looks like my younger brother." The laughter continued. After a week, most of the students in the class had shaved their heads. It took Jean a bit longer to take off her wig. She felt accepted.

The only person, who was not at the gravesite, was the town's Doctor. Shirley a young, first-time-to-be mother was in the last stages of labour at Civic Hospital in Peterborough. Dr. Atkinson had to be there. Manley and Dr. Atkinson were the best of friends and they would reconnect later. Dr. Atkinson had been the town's only town doctor when Jake came into the world. Jake did not need a tap on the bum. He came out crying. One thing that the town did not know was that Jake was the son of a young teenage girl. He was born out of wedlock.

He was born in the same early morning hours as Rose. Jake would be the first son, of this young teenager from a well-established farm family in Westwood. This young mother had no means to raise a child. Her parents were typical parents, embarrassed that their daughter was pregnant, but not able to afford to send her to private school or just away. Instead she had been sent to live with her aunt on a farm near Millbrook to hide the pregnancy.

Most small-town family doctors looked after everyone in their communities. The teenage girl was told quietly by Doctor Atkinson that the baby was going to be looked after and a family had been found. Rose's parents had been given the option of taking home two babies, instead of one, and they agreed with the doctor's plan. Paternal twins do not always look alike especially when they are female and male. Only the doctor, Shirley, her parents, and the operating nurse knew the true story. The records were sealed away.

The official part of the funeral was over. The people in earshot were invited back to the basement of the United Church to visit with family and friends and enjoy a light lunch. Close friends, family and people from out-of-town congregated in the church basement and enjoyed egg, tuna, salmon, and ground meat sandwiches. Platters of cheese and vegetables were placed on the serving table and coffee and tea were served by the ladies hosting the luncheon. A reasonable fee was charged to the family for this luncheon.

Annie, an elderly town lady, attended every luncheon. All funerals, weddings, anniversaries, and birthday receptions had a place for Annie. In some cases Annie knew only the serving staff but they would make her feel comfortable. She was part of the town and this was her outing for the week, a lunch or a dinner that she did not have to prepare and eat alone in her small home. Annie did not know Jake, but she knew his parents and many of his relatives were familiar faces and they would pass the time of day with her. Annie was an integral part of the fabric of Norwood.

Everyone who knew Jake now had a hole to fill. Cleaning out the school locker, cleaning out his bedroom, collecting all the small possessions that were a part of Jake was hard to do. You can't say goodbye; you only hope to understand. Jake is not here and we are left. Are we the lucky ones and will this happen to us again? The answer is yes. If you live long enough, you get to see it all. If you live long enough, you lose all your older relatives, your neighbours, your friends, and, maybe if luck is with you, your memory.

The dirt was shovelled back into the hole. The sod was placed and tramped on top and the job was done. One of Jake's school buddies stayed behind. He could not leave his buddy alone. Only when darkness fell did he leave and walk home slowly. Hank was with Jake to the end.

Jean saw Hank walking past their house towards the highway, where he would hitch a ride. She found her dad and asked him if he could take the car and give Hank a lift.

A week after the funeral, Manley was in the doctor's office for his yearly medical. Only a few people in town had a yearly medical, but Manley always requested one. He wanted to be in control of his life, and to do that, he had to be in control of his body. He was one of the few people whom Doctor Atkinson had met in town to hold this belief. Manley thought of his body as a machine that had to be maintained, properly fed, rested, worked, and cared for. He also thought that his mind ought to be kept active and challenged to keep growing. Dr. Atkinson prepared for this medical. The questions Manley would ask would probe into the current research and views, not only of North American medical practices, but also of others, such as the veterinarian school in Guelph.

Manley had read the death notice posted on the corner hydro pole at the four corners of town. The date: Born April 2, 1945 jumped out at Manley as he recognized the numbers and remembered his younger brother had a son born out of wedlock on that same day, same year.

Young blood runs hot and Manley's brother, Richard, in one of his rare uncontrolled moments had stepped over the line and a pregnancy was the result. Richard usually had a dating standard that above the waist was fair game, but not to touch or go below the belt. One night during a hot July spell, one slip in the back of a 1952 Ford.

Manley looked directly at Dr. Atkinson and asked the question that he had been waiting fourteen years to answer. "Was Jake, Richard and Shirley's son?" Doctors do not take a lying course in medical school, but they all must master this art early in their careers. Some patients cannot take bad news and others need to be misled. There is no need to cause patients more danger or more pain.

Dr. Atkinson paused, looked down, and then went into the routine he had practised for years. He looked Manley straight in the eye and said, "I have been waiting for years for you to put things together and ask this question. Manley, you are one of my best friends and I have to tell you, Jake was not your brothers' son." When the examination was over, Manley dressed and got ready to leave the prep room.

On leaving, he turned to Dr. Atkinson and said, "When you looked me in the eye, your pupils told the story. You are a true friend." He quietly closed the door behind himself, walked to the parking lot, and drove home.

Dr. Atkinson had given Manley a diagnosis for his condition. Manley was showing early signs of dementia, known later as a disease, like Alzheimer's. Manley had forgotten that his memory was fading. His hunting error in judgment was due to the onset of his illness. Manley was one of the lucky ones, as his disease progressed slowly, and he had a number of ways to compensate for memory loss. The one thing he did do, was to tell everyone what he was suffering of and then he asked for their support and understanding. As the elected reeve of Norwood he got both.

Epilogue

Dr. Atkinson explained to Manley that the mind plays tricks as it slowly disintegrates. You lose trust in people whom you have known all your life. You forget details. Your mind makes up stories. You are not sure if it was a dream or did it really happen.

Manley was showing early signs of dementia and, if he was lucky, it would progress slowly.

Just before Manley left the doctor's office, he asked Dr. Atkinson why he had not been at the funeral.

Dr. Atkinson said, "What funeral?"

Dr. Atkinson then asked Manley if he was going on the hunt this year. Dr. Atkinson, with all the practice he had, held his smile as he observed the face of an old man wash across Manley's complexion. Fear started leaking out of his eyes.

Manley was confused and he knew he had to go straight home and ask his wife, Cora, a lot of important questions.

Chapter Two

Sniper World War II

Manley was on a downward spiral of guilt, and Rose's small, warm hand asking for help saved him from walking down the road of suicide that day.

Manley, like many people among those gathered at the cemetery, drifted off into his own world, as the Reverend said all the right things. Manley's last mission in Germany at the end of the Second World War flashed through his mind. This life experience had surfaced frequently in dreams, but never before during daylight hours.

Manley, a sniper during the Second World War, was the best his regiment had. Manley had grown up with a rifle. He shot groundhogs, rabbits, partridges, and all kinds of small game, and in every weather condition imaginable. During the war years, many farm boys with good shooting skills were identified and channelled quickly into unique sniping corps.

When the call to join the forces came, Manley was screened from the pack at the rifle range. Most farm kids were good with rifles and scored well at the target range, but Manley was different. The poster man, down in the butts, was marking the holes in the target, pasting the holes as the shots were fired. In Manley's case, his target had only one hole, as each shell went dead centre into the same hole. Before the farm lads started at the target range, Sergeant Adams had every recruit put five dollars into a prize bucket to be given for the best marks of the day. This was to be Sergeant Adams' drinking money for the next couple of weeks. To his utter surprise, he could not come close to Manley's score that day.

Manley, and a number of other farm kids, were selected to enrol in sniper training school after they completed basic training.

To be a sniper and hunt down and kill another human being is a mental challenge for most. Manley was able to do the job, because he was so loyal to his friends and regiment. He wanted soldiers to finish their service and return home to families, communities, and work. The only way to stop enemies was to disable them completely or to end their lives.

During his military service, Manley was called on a number of times to take out certain targets. He would leave camp unannounced and return after the mission. Snipers worked by themselves and kept to themselves. They were amongst the few people during a conflict that would actually study and see the enemy before taking them out. Killing was not easy and a sniper would have to psych himself up to be able to pull the trigger. Manley always told himself that if he did not take out the enemy, his friends and the officers of his regiment would continue to be killed.

In the early fall of 1944, Manley was called to go on a special mission. The Hastings Prince Edward Regiment, an infantry regiment, was busy and they needed an expert. In the march towards Germany, an entire division was bogged down, taking a large number of casualties due to sniper fire. All the snipers sent out to get rid of the problem had not returned. Some were found dead and some were not found at all. A sniper to take out a sniper was required. After assessing the risk, Manley volunteered to leave his regiment and go on the mission. He saluted Captain Adams and was on his way.

Manley was flown, trucked, and marched into camp, where he was briefed on his assignment. The first thing the commanding officer noticed was that Manley was different from any of the previous snipers. Manley grilled him, his officers, and everyone else in camp with hundreds of questions. Manley was only interested in those snipers who had been sent out and who had not returned...their personalities, how they walked, how they talked, their ages, where they came from, and all of their personal idiosyncrasies. Manley was drawing a profile of the dead snipers. He knew that he was up against the best. A sniper taking out snipers is like a cop catching a bad cop.

Once Manley had acquired all the information he could gather, he put together the tools and supplies that would be required for a two-week trip. In the past, he had only planned for being away one week. This time it would be different.

Moving out in the early evening as darkness fell, Manley took advantage of the excellent maps provided. He could see where the enemy lines and pockets of soldiers might be holding out. Moving in the shadows and keeping downwind, he slowly advanced to the front line. Daylight hours were spent under a shed, a wagon, a log. He did not move during the day. It took two days to get near the front. He could only smell and sense it. He could not see what was ahead.

On the third evening, dressed in dark clothes and with his skin soiled with sand and mud, Manley crawled up to see the camp ahead.

On the way to the front, he had passed a farm that was surprisingly similar to the farm where he grew up as a child. German barns were excellent structures and had been copied and built throughout southern Ontario. Manley's plan was to attract attention and retreat to this barn where he would set a trap for the sniper he was hunting. The trick was to survive both setting the trap and the retreat.

After assessing what he had to do to get attention, he slowly made his way back to the farm to set up his ambush. The first job was to get the horses, cows, pigs, chickens, and other livestock familiar with his smell and his presence. He did not want disturbed animals signalling his location. Watching the family operation, he saw the daily pattern to their chores. No seat by the farm boots meant that only women and children were working the stock. Milking times, feeding times, manure cleanout, were all carefully noted. The two small children who worked and played with two women were a delight, and added other ideas to his task. The barn was almost identical to the barn back in Norwood, Manley's hometown. The two haymows, the granary, the hay chute from the haymow above to the downstairs' livestock level, the pens, and the cow stalls were also familiar. The stalls for the cows and the bull stall beside the stairs were the same as those he knew from the farm in Norwood. The barn's cement floor had a trough-like gutter that took each cow's manure and urine to a side wall and that was also in the same location as back home.

Manley spent four days watching and studying the movement of the family and the schedule for doing chores.

Manley had never hunted another sniper and certainly not one who had been successful in taking out other snipers. He knew he was up against an expert, or maybe there were two snipers working together. Snipers never worked in pairs, but this could be the exception. Manley decided to set up the ambush for two and possibly three men. He did not know at the time that he was up against identical twins who had worked together for over four years and had notched their weapons many times. These twins were from a small town in Bavaria and were the third generation in a family of butchers. Each twin was extremely fit, carrying the upper body strength of a working butcher, and was no match for a normal man. In the past, hand-to-hand combat had meant a quick kill. Using a knife on a human was easier that using a knife on a cold animal carcass in the butcher shop.

Under the hay chute, which was used to drop hay from the second floor to the ground floor, Manley planted a manure fork with its handle down and six tines pointing upwards into the hayloft. Anyone sliding down the chute would land on the pointed prongs of the fork. The two side-support arms of the hay chute were greased with teat cream. This would prevent a person sliding down from swinging himself out to the side of the hay chute, and instead, he would land on top of the soiled manure fork. Six long fork prongs stood at attention when Manley was finished.

Many times at home, Manley had helped his dad use a chunk of rope to upend cows to clip their hooves or to fix other problems, so he was experienced in setting ropes to topple the biggest cows. A skipping rope left behind by the two children would do the trick. Placing the rope loosely under and around the breeding stall would be enough to pull the hind feet of a cow and tip her over. All but one of the stalls was the same size. Back home, the slightly larger one was used when a cow was getting close to calving. The extra room was needed for someone to get in beside the expectant mother. Manley placed the skipping rope on the floor of the larger stall and strung it back to the gateway beside the bull's stall. That's where Manley would be waiting patiently.

Everything was in place. The cats and farm dog had become accustomed to Manley. When the family was not in the barn, the animals liked the stroking and nudging, a pat here, a stroke there, and a handful of feed always did the trick.

To get attention and draw the sniper or snipers out, Manley knew he would have to take out an officer or some other important target. In the darkness and under the protection of a steady fall wind, Manley approached the enemy camp and took up his position. Snipers know that they only get one shot and it had better be on the mark. Cold-blooded killing was one option or a near miss would be just as effective to get attention.

Cooks are protected and prized in the field as everyone wants to come back and eat well. Shoot the cook and everyone will be after you seeking revenge. The planned shot was fired. It grazed the cook's hat. To Manley's great surprise, the bullet continued on, hitting the storage area behind the cook. That storage happened to contain gas cooking cylinders. The resulting explosion not only wrecked the kitchen but also killed the assistant cook and two officers eating a late supper. Someone saw the direction the rifle fire had come from and the hunt was on.

Manley retreated to the farm and waited. He knew that to set up his ambush the family had to be out of the barn when the sniper or snipers, if there were two, arrived to hunt him down. Manley was hoping that no innocent person would be in the way.

Every time the family left the barn, Manley set up his ambush, and each time when they were to return, Manley would remove the props. He did not want to snare the children or the two women operating the farm.

On the second evening after the kitchen fire, Manley thought he saw shadows moving his way. He had a pair of old eye glasses that he had saved. In the moonlight he made the lenses reflect light by poking the spectacles out of the top of the end granary. Whoever was out there would see the reflection off the glasses and would assume that his prey was in the top floor of the barn. This night, one brother signalled that he would go in the top and the other brother was to circle and go in the south end of the lower floor. If that door was not open, he would have to crawl through the open manure chute.

Manley had planned on leaving a lantern burning slowly on the wire that ran along the front of the cow stalls, but that night's moon cast enough light as it shone through the lower windows.

He heard one person enter the north barn door on the second floor and waited for the second or third person.

The stairs leading down from the mows to the main barn floor were the open type and worn with age. Manley had practiced standing under them and, using his hand, made them squeak as if a person was walking up or down. Manley had used this trick many times before in Norwood when he played hide and go seek in the barn with his cousins.

Every inch of this barn was a story. This time it was a game of hide and go seek, for keeps.

Manley reached up and pulled on the steps one after the other. There was no question that it sounded like someone was walking down the stairs.

Manley was prepared for a second sniper entering the ground floor. He thought this sniper might enter by the south door or, if he was very crafty, he might come through the manure door that was at the end of the gutter leading out to the manure pile. A shiny milk pail was positioned against the west wall, so Manley would be able to see someone come in to the lower part of the stable. He saw a figure crawl into the first stall at the south end. Now, if he would only advance and move into the larger stall where the kids had left the milk stool. The skipping rope was in place.

The creaking of the stairs informed the lower sniper that it was safe to move further into the building. He advanced four stalls closer to the stairs and slid into the stall beside the cow and the empty milking stool.

There is a judgment call on when to pull the surprise. Seconds ticked by and Manley knew the two soldiers were adjusting their eyes to the available light and were waiting for him to make another move. The twins had been in similar situations before and their teamwork had proven effective, time and time again.

Manley heard the faint steps of the sniper above. The first sniper was gliding across the loft floor to the hay chute, probably thinking that he could slide down quickly to catch his enemy by surprise, hopefully within knife or handgun range.

Within a heartbeat, Manley heard the first sniper slide down the ramp. There was a soft thud as the sniper lost his grip and slid down the greased hay chute right onto the manure fork. A manure fork standing on end is taller than a man's legs. The sniper looked down and felt the prongs enter his body. Six manure fork prongs went into his abdomen. He knew he was dying and fainted from fear and panic. For a moment, he was perfectly balanced on the fork, but then he toppled into the cow stall in front of the larger stall. The second sniper heard the motion and the sigh and he tensed. The cow beside him shuffled. Manley pulled the end of the skipping rope to upset this eight-hundred pound cow. The rope took the hind feet out from under the cow and she dropped onto her side. Under the cow, pinched up against the side of the wood frame, was the second sniper.

The twins came into the world together and they left together.

His job was done. On the way out of the lower west door, Manley saw the second sniper's arm outstretched into the gutter.

Ironically, it was this cow's calf that had been taken a week before to be butchered for meat by the German camp. These two snipers had themselves selected and butchered the heifer, as food was in short supply and breeding stock was being sacrificed to feed the troops when necessary.

Manley never stopped looking for the third sniper.

As usual, no one asked and no one was told. Manley informed the commanding officer that his job was done and he would like to be reassigned back to his own regiment.

Chapter Three

Sometimes Teenagers Bump Into Love

Many people have great ideas and some of these lead to great inventions. The thinking processes in both creating something new and then making the idea work are the first crucial steps in heading down the trail to success or failure. This concept is illustrated in the story of Rose Payne, her husband Everett English, and their friends Ruthie and Bruce.

Rose, Jake's twin sister, had the unique ability of knowing where her body space started and stopped. As a young child growing up, she never bumped into anything, never dropped anything, and not even spilled a glass of milk. She could see and sense the flow of people, animals, trucks, cars, and just about anything that moved.

Rose's favourite game was to make people trip up, stumble, or feel awkward at any given time. Every person has had the experience of going through a doorway and almost bumping into someone, when the clues for left and right foul up and both people end up going in the same direction. A collision can only be averted at the last minute. Rose could trigger those moments at will, and put anyone she pleased in a gangly position.

Rose met Everett in her second year at NDHS, Norwood District High School. Everett was the opposite of Rose. He would trip on smooth grass, bump into filing cabinets, knock over glasses of beer, and drop and break the finest of china.

Everett was nicknamed "Lightning" by his friends. Everett got his first nickname from his hockey buddies. They all knew, by playing shinny and then hockey in an arena, that they would be struck. Everett bumped into everyone and he loved it. A big smile, stretched all over his face, all the time that was Everett. When you didn't expect it, he would hit you and it felt like a bolt of lightning. Then came the big smile.

The only thing he was skilled at was playing hockey, if he was on defence. Rushing forwards could not get around him, as he was always in their way. If they tried a head fake, body fake, or any other method to slip by, Everett did not pick up the clues. He just eyed their chests and stumbled in front of them. In the corners behind the net, he crushed his opposition, as what fun is hockey if you can't hit and hit hard. He had the corners to himself, as few experienced players wanted to sit on the bench protecting wounds for the rest of the game. Their injuries were not permanent, but they were visible in the dressing room when the equipment came off.

There was one exception to inflicting superficial injuries, and it happened during a game with the Havelock bantams. Brian, a defenseman on the Havelock team, had the dirty habit of taking the heel of his hockey stick and chopping the ankles of high goal scorers on the opposing team. This Wednesday night, the two referees, one from Havelock and one from Norwood, were not picking up on the dirt. Norwood's top scorer, Rick, was getting chopped and his ankles were getting too sore to skate. Ian, their goal tender, was a talker and ran the game on the ice. Goalies are either silent or they are talkers. Ian was a talker and he told everyone what was going on.

During the second period intermission, while the ice was being flooded, Ian, Rick, and Lightning decided to play the old snow-bank trick on Brian, only in an arena with boards and no soft snow banks. These old Norwood pond pals would settle the score.

Back on the ice and midway through the third period, Rick put the puck on Brian's stick at the Norwood blue line. Brian took the bait and rushed the goalie. He didn't see Everett switch sides with the other defenseman. When he got close to the net, he finally looked up, and when he saw Everett's big smile, he knew he was in trouble. He had no idea how much trouble. Everett body-checked him cleanly, and as Brian slid, the goalie's stick steered him past the steel post but headfirst into the boards. Then he felt a bag of rocks, that seemed to have elbows and knees, fall on him and ride him, left shoulder first, into the boards. The rink crowd were on their feet. The crunch into the boards and a snap could be heard across the arena. A dislocated shoulder and a broken arm took Brian out for the rest of the season. The referees knew they had let the game get out of control and that players had taken over their job. Brian Senior, watching from the stands, wished for the first time in his life that he had not passed the family propensity for dirty tricks onto his son.

In the dressing rooms after the game, both rooms were quiet until Rick spoke up, and in front of the team and coach, he pointed to Lightning, and said, "In Havelock they will be calling you Thunder." A quick wink and a big smile and nothing else had to be said.

Monday morning at their lockers in Norwood District High School, Ian and Brian were three feet apart. Brian had his shoulder in a sling and his arm in a cast. He turned to Ian and said, "Is Everett going to forgive me?" They both started to laugh. They would later play football together and have fun beating up on other teams and getting even for past bruises. That is another story.

Rose was in grade ten. Walking down the hall on the first week of school in her second year, she saw a tall, long drink of water, a grade nine student walking towards her. He would be fair game. This would be fun. She would play her trick on this boy and, with any luck at all, he would bump into a locker trying to get around her. She gave the clue and moved to one side to watch him stumble by, but he didn't. He ran right into her, put both arms around her, and squeezed her in a bear hug. Everett was on defence and had just stopped another player. He excused himself and continued down the hall. For the first time in her life, Rose was at a loss to explain why he had not been fooled like everyone else before him. She had to know his name.

He grew up on a dairy farm outside Norwood and had two older brothers, one older sister, and twin younger sisters. His older siblings were in grade thirteen, grade twelve, and grade eleven. His twin sisters were in public school in Hastings. Rose checked to see on which bus he came to school, as most students at Norwood were bussed in from Havelock, Hastings, Westwood, Centre Dummer, Trent River, Donegal, Killarney Corners, Cordova Mines, or Cottesloe. These communities put the word district in NDHS.

Shinny was hockey played on a pond. Everyone played together no matter the age. For equipment, all you needed was one stick and warm clothing, no helmet, no pads. Rules were simple. No raising the puck, if someone could get hit. When you got tired and needed a rest, you found a snow bank to fall into. The goal posts were two boots spread apart at each end of the ice rink, and the better team would have their boots farther apart. No icing the puck for a goal, and no adults or referees allowed. Older players settled all disputes, which were few and far between. Shinny was hockey and was played for hours, until it was time to go home. On cold days someone would always bring a tire and start a bonfire at the edge of the pond, where everyone sat up wind to put on their skates. When players took a break, they would go and put more branches on the fire to keep it going. For many young boys, "Canada's Golden Pond," is frozen and there is a "real" hockey net at each end.

Everett always found something to laugh at, or someone to laugh with, and just about everything was a new discovery. If his dad took him into the hardware store, grocery store, or any other store, Everett would disappear. He had to touch, handle, and play with anything that he had not seen before. One Saturday morning at the Blatchford Feed Mill, Everett wandered into the warehouse looking at all the chicken-feeding and watering equipment. When his dad finished loading some ground corn chop, he drove home. Everett was not missed until lunchtime, when everyone sat down to eat and noticed that his seat was empty. Everett's mom asked, "Where is Everett?" As she spoke, Everett's dad remembered that he had left him back at the mill in Norwood. The mill closed at noon on Saturdays and, sure enough, there was Everett sitting on the loading platform waiting for his dad. The workers at the mill realized what had happened. The office manager said he would wait for Everett's dad to pick him up, or he would call and drive him home himself.

Rose was interested in Everett and the dating game was on. Everett didn't know he was being stalked. In high school it is a rare occurrence that an older girl will date a younger boy. This was an exception to the rule, as Rose was curious.

The first sock hop of the year would be held the third week in September. Sock hops were school dances held on Fridays at 4 o'clock. On dance days, school buses were held back until 9 p.m. At NDHS most students were bussed, so for these dances almost every student was in the gym with socks on waiting to dance or hoping to avoid being asked to dance. The total student population of NDHS came in at about three hundred and fifty. Usually, out of five grade nine classes that started high school, one class of grade thirteen students actually completed high school. Lunch was served at six in the school cafeteria, the midpoint of the sock hop. Evert was not sure why they called a cold snack at six lunch but lunch or dinner he was not going to complain about a name. Home economics classes made all the sandwiches, cheese platters, and pickle bowls. A seventy-five cent admission fee to the dance covered the cost of food. Since farm and mining kids eat a lot, the food committee estimated the amount of food needed to feed five grade nine classes, four grade ten's, three grade eleven's, two grade twelve's, and one grade thirteen class. Calculating that half of the students were girls and half boys, the food committee estimated the total food they would need. Their teacher, Mrs. Turpine, would always tell them to add fifty percent. They always ran out. After a sock hop, every student went home to raid the pantry.

Farm students would get home between nine-thirty and ten p.m. and quickly change their clothes before heading to the barn to do their chores. On those late dance nights, their usual after-school chores would be switched to ones that could be done later when they got home. The idea of having to do no chores, even after coming home so late, was never considered. Everyone was needed on a farm.

One of the senior boys, nicknamed Tiny, finally danced at this first sock hop of the year. It took him only four years to get up enough courage to get on the dance floor. Afterwards, he mentioned to his friends that he had asked Joan out for a date on Saturday. Actually, this information was very carefully pried out of him. A first date could be made memorable. He and Joan would be going to a movie on George Street in Peterborough. This was a rare opportunity to pull a prank on Tiny, as he had been responsible for so many others.

Tiny just happened to be the largest grade-thirteen boy in the school. What else would you call him?

On Sunday mornings Tiny drove his sister and parents to church. His dad sat in the front seat and his mom and sister sat in the back seat of the Dodge. Unknown to Tiny, late Saturday night in the farm laneway, the football guys placed a large bra under the blanket in the back seat of the car, just behind the driver where Tiny's mom always sat. The strap was left dangling out, just enough to be seen. A few years later at his stag, Tiny would find out who had set him up for the most embarrassing moment of his life. The story, by the best man, brought down the house.

Rose was going to find Everett at the first dance and start her plan. The dance started at four. Students drifted into the gym, with girls sitting on metal chairs along the west wall and boys sitting on the chairs along the east wall. Rose scanned the row of guys. Everett was not there. He was at his locker cleaning out all his books and binders. Everett had decided that his locker needed to be better organized, and brought some pre-measured boards and hooks to redesign his twelve-inch by sixty-three inch space. He knew his coat was exactly thirty-two inches long and his boots were seven inches high. The top shelf held all the textbooks for his eight classes. This was a chance to build-in shelves to keep his binders out of the water and slush that would happen in the winter. Everett had the perfect shelving solution for a school locker.

When other students noticed Everett's locker, they were amazed at how much junk he could store and they asked him if he would help them do their lockers. Everett, a budding entrepreneur, realized that a few boards would generate a few bucks. He was very good at explaining that he had to get the lumber, machine it to size for each locker, and that it would cost something. At two bucks a locker, Everett was in business. Two bucks was enough to go to the Riverside Dance Pavilion, and have a milkshake for two afterwards.

Everett finally wandered into the dance at five and found an empty chair down the wall. He would have been very happy to sit and talk to his buddies until break time, but a bingo dance was in progress. He didn't hear the student council rep yell "Bingo", and there was Rose asking him to dance. Everett didn't recognize Rose from their previous bump experience in the hall, as he had stumbled into a thousand people before. Everett hated dancing. Every time he had to get up, he stepped on feet, elbowed into other couples, and wished he was on his dad's new tractor out in the woods.

Get this over as quickly as possible was his motto.

This time it was different. A slow song was on. Perhaps, it was "Sleep Walk." He got up reluctantly to dance. Everett did not want to say no to anyone. They got on the floor and the first thing that Everett looked for was how much room there was around him. Oh God, a slow dance. The floor would be full. Everett did not realize that he was with Rose. She carefully guided him around the dance floor, stayed out of the way of his footsteps, and made him into the perfect dancer. This was the first time he had not bumped into someone, stepped on his partner, or felt extremely awkward.

At the end of the record, he was stunned. In the past he would have said, "Thank you", and headed for the chairs to get the evening over with. Now, he looked into Rose's eyes and said, "That is the first time I enjoyed dancing. Could we do that again some time?" Everett, not realizing that Rose would like to continue dancing with him now, thanked her, and went back to his seat.

At break time in the cafeteria, boys and girls sat together to eat, not like at the dance when boys sat against the north wall and girls against the south. Everett's group of friends and Rose's group of friends were at the same table, and it just so happened that Rose and Everett ended up sitting across from each other. Everett could pack the sandwiches away and lay waste to the pickle and cheese tray. Conversation was all around. Everett watched Rose. She was fun. She was chatty and had a great sense of timing and humour. He had never heard a girl tell jokes, and Rose had plenty.

Everett noticed that whenever he was with Rose, he didn't bump into, trip, or knock over a thing. Rose knew where to be and where to position herself so Everett would not fumble. They started eating together at lunch time in the cafeteria, which was a first, as the girls ate on one side and the boys ate on the other side. This pattern was also the way seating was structured for Wednesday morning assemblies. Girls sat on the right side of the stage and boys sat on the left side. Students were accustomed to lining up at separate doors before entering elementary schools, but in high school boys and girls were allowed to use the same doors for the first time. They were still required to walk single file in the halls between classes.

At the end of a school day, Rose took her bus back to Westwood and Everett got on his bus that went to Hastings. In the morning, Rose's bus arrived minutes before Everett's and she always found a reason to be there when Everett got off his bus. Many mornings they just walked together. Everett always gave Rose a bump before they went off to their own lockers to start the day. Since Everett was in grade nine and Rose was in ten, they did not have any classes together, but they knew when they would cross paths between classes. Lunch time was thirty-five minutes and they would sit together with their group of friends and laugh, talk, and tell stories.

When Rose turned sixteen, she got her sixty-day temporary licence, and shortly after that passed her driver's test in Campbellford for her permanent license. Everett was fifteen and waiting for his day to arrive.

In the summer, Riverside Dance Pavilion in Hastings was the place to be on Saturday nights. Everett would get a ride from his brother Harvey or a friend and Rose would be there. Rose was trusted to drive the second and oldest family pickup to the dance with her girlfriends, and they would all show up together for the dance. After the dance, Rose dropped off her girlfriends at their homes, and then she would circle back and pick up Everett. They had their favourite parking spot and would get in at least an hour of good necking before it was time to go home. Rose would drop Everett off at his farm mailbox, and she would put the Chevy pickup in her family's drive shed just before curfew.

When Everett turned sixteen he got his own driver's licence and wheels.

Everett had the use of the second family car, a nineteen fifty-three Chevrolet, four-door. The family had two Chevies because the 1953 Chevy had no trade in value. It was so badly rusted that his dad just kept it for spare parts. The three-speed standard or "three-on-the-tree" had seen better days. The floor was rusted through in a number of places and the fenders were just about falling off. The car ran though, and for two bucks worth of gas, it could get Everett most places he wanted to go.

Double-dating was the rule most of the time and gas costs were split. It was more fun that way. Rose's best girlfriend Ruthie and her friend Bruce were the couple they double-dated with most often. When Ruthie turned seventeen, she made a decision that made it impossible for the foursome to continue. Ruthie, an attractive five-foot-two bundle of energy wanted sex. With another couple in the front or back-seat of the same car, it was not going to be private.

Ruthie told Rose about the conversation that she had with Bruce. Ruthie had put down dating rules. No smoking and no drinking, but within a half hour of being picked up she wanted to have sex, and after the movie or dance she wanted sex before going home. As she said to Rose, "You don't have to drink or smoke to have fun." Bruce was happy to oblige and stated his requirements. He told Ruthie he loved to fish, and every Sunday during the season they were going fishing.

Before meeting Bruce, Ruthie made a rule that she would not date any boy who did not have sisters. She found out that guys who grew up without sisters spent too much time necking and playing around with things and she wanted to get down to business. Bruce was constantly amazed that no matter what truck or car they were in, Ruthie knew how to move. This was her bedroom, and he was happy to follow.

Ruthie dragged Bruce into back seats and Bruce dragged Ruthie down every creek, river, and lake in the Kawarthas and beyond. Every Sunday afternoon Bruce would light up the small portable barbeque on the tailgate of his half-ton and a fresh fish dinner would be washed down with a couple of cold beers. Trout, pickerel, bass, mud cat, and pan fish all tasted great at the end of the day. They both were hooked on each other's sport. On many occasions they would be surprised out of their skins. They would be in the backwoods down a stream and all by themselves sitting quietly enticing a trout to take their bait and they would get a light tap on their shoulder. They could never figure out how Joe could sneak up behind. After their heart beat settled down they would check to see that he had not dropped in on Tarzan's rope. Joe and Bruce would in later years team up and become a formidable force in the Pro Bass fishing tournaments. Joe always seemed to know the days that they would have no luck and sure enough he would show up with a mouth-watering catch.

Bruce loved to sail and got hooked on ice sailing. In the early winter and after a winter's melt, conditions could be perfect for ice sailing. Ice has to be thick enough to carry the sailor and an ice boat and the surface must be clear and smooth enough for the skates to cut into the ice. Skates on the bottom of a boat work the same as skates on feet. Friction between the metal blade and the ice creates heat and the blade rides on a thin film of water. This explains why on a very cold day, at minus twenty-five or colder, it is difficult to skate. A warm day, just at freezing, makes for the easiest skate.

Bruce and his buddy Harold, who was an auctioneer, built their own ice boats. These were put up on blocks, ready to go when conditions were perfect. Sails were stored inside and were ready to be rigged at a moment's notice. Some years their boats never got off the blocks, while other years they would get two or three days in the fall and four or five outings in the spring's thaw-freeze cycle. Their favourite lake to sail was Pigeon Lake, as it was about twenty miles long and west winds funnelled down the Omemee hills straight along the lake. North winds went the opposite direction. They just wanted a smooth, safe surface and a wind. Somehow, Bruce and Harold always negotiated their holiday time to be "on call" for those days when ice and wind were perfect. No day job was going to get in their way for a few perfect days of ice sailing.

When they were out on the frozen lake cutting across from shoreline to shoreline, Bruce and Harold were thinking about speed and the sound of quiet skates cutting the surface, hoping they would feel a gust and be able to ride it, and not let it go by for fear of tipping. They were very conscious of the dangerous parts. Open water, pressure ridges, stumps, and rocks had to be avoided at all costs. When the temperature changed and the lake was making ice, or when the water levels dropped in a lake, forming a water basin for the spring runoff, surface conditions could change quickly. Bruce and Harold each carried a life preserver and a long floating ski rope, with a pre-made slipknot at one end, in case of emergencies. They feared drifting into open water and going down.

Snowmobiles were gaining in popularity and the six and eight-horsepower machines were heavy and did not turn well on ice. Although the sport was originally called skidooing, Bombardier realized that if they did not change this term, they would lose the trade name of Skidoo, so they instructed their franchise outlets and dealers to advertise and broadcast the sport as "snowmobiling".

This was long before carbide ski-runners and machines with power and speed that could easily run on water. Inexperienced riders were common, helmets, snowmobile mitts, boots and other equipment were not yet developed in the early nineteen-sixties.

One Sunday morning in early spring, the boys were ice sailing on Chemong Lake, just north of Peterborough. A week-long thaw, followed by three-day deep freeze, and an inch of light snow dropped on the countryside, made this a near-perfect day for sailing. They knew the treacherous weak spots along the causeway where the water flowed under the roadway in huge culverts, unseen from above. Close to the causeway was the most dangerous place to be, as culverts moved water from one side of the road to the other. Where the water flowed, the surface ice became thinner and thinner and would not support either an ice boat or a slow-moving snowmobile.

They were on the north side of the causeway that Sunday, when Bruce and Harold saw two riders on a snowmobile heading east across the lake right next to the causeway. In an instant, they knew that the riders were in trouble, because at the end of the causeway, the ice under the bridge was as thin as wax paper.

Bruce signalled Harold. There was no question that the machine and the two riders were going in. The snowmobilers would be about fifty to seventy-five feet away from the causeway with no way to get to land. If they were lucky to avoid the culverts, they would end up at the bridge and fall in where the water current was stronger. The only way the machine would avoid going in was if the riders turned east and headed down the lake, as the ice there was much thicker and safer for a snowmobile and a passenger. If they stayed on their present course along the causeway, they would go in as soon as they slowed down. If they did not slow down, they were going in under the bridge.

Ice sailing near or under the bridge would be difficult. Bruce and Harold knew that they would have to sail past the snowmobile, dragging their rope lines, and then crash into the side of the causeway, hopefully, in an area that had strong-enough ice to support their crafts. Having enough speed to get across the thin ice and to the causeway, yet being able to pull up without crashing, would be tricky at best. They would have only one chance each to get a line to the people in the water. They would have to work quickly as warm-blooded humans have only a few minutes in icy water before they start to lose consciousness and can't think, let alone grab a line. Hopefully, the slip knots they always tied to the ends of their ropes would catch and lock on a hand or arm and the person would be pulled out of the freezing water to safety.

Bruce and Harold hovered slightly upwind waiting for the yellow snow machine to go through the ice. Sure enough, about halfway along the causeway, about eighty feet from shore, the snowmobile stopped. The rear passenger pulled out a camera. They had stopped to take a picture of the two ice boats. The machine and two riders did not sink slowly. They dropped out of sight like a stone.

Bruce caught the wind first and dragged his rope over the two swimmers. Harold followed closely behind, putting his rope in the same position. The two swimmers grabbed a rope each and the slip knots worked. They were tied to the end of the rope. Both ice boats and sailors ended up on the side of the causeway with a minimum amount of damage. They were well-enough anchored for the small crowd to haul in two very cold, wet riders. A number of cars had stopped on the causeway to offer help. The lucky couple was pulled out and loaded into a warm half-ton truck before they realized that their lives had been saved.

Until he looked into the truck, Bruce did not know that they had pulled Ruthie`s youngest brother, Ike, and his new girlfriend, Judy, out of the icy water of Chemong Lake. The snowmobile would be recovered in warmer weather. Ruthie had been the one who asked her brother to capture some action shots of Bruce and Harold ice-sailing.

Both Bruce and Harold made a few minor adjustments on their ice boats before heading back onto the lake. The excitement of sailing was gone for both of them for that day and they headed back to the landing to pack their gear and go home. They were mentally exhausted and both fell into their beds when they got home. They did not know that they were heroes.

Adventures in ice sailing were plentiful for Bruce and Harold.

The closest they came to killing a human being was on Pigeon Lake in late fall, during an early winter freeze-up. Pigeon Lake is unique. This large, shallow lake freezes up quickly in the fall, and melts just as quickly in the spring. Every year, good sailing ice forms first at Pigeon, but few sailors know this, and those who do, keep it a secret. Ice sailors on Pigeon have to be careful of the river out of Bobcaygeon, Gannon's Narrows, the Emily Park current, and the drain from Bald Lakes. Everywhere else is safe and there are miles and miles of solid ice.

The year was nineteen sixty-three. Cold winter winds were moving in. Because Pigeon Lake is shallow and does not have a cold thermal turn over it freezes quickly. Because it has few currents, it is safe for sailing. On November eleventh, the lake was covered in two inches of black ice and the temperature was going down. This could be a good year for early sailing. A friend of Harold's in Peterborough had a bread truck route that serviced the stores around the Kawartha Lakes. He always kept Harold posted on ice conditions.

It was a special year and by November eighteenth there were seven inches of black ice on Pigeon Lake. After Harold checked and measured the ice in several spots, he phoned his sailing buddy Bruce, and they started to pack. Trailers were loaded; clothing, food, and safety equipment were checked and double-checked.

When you go ice sailing, you have a number of things on your mind. You have to watch for stumps, rock shoals, and especially, pressure ridges. Pressure ridges form when ice freezes and a fault line forms. Water expands about ten percent when frozen and, whether in a lake or in an ice cube tray, frozen water rises. The shoreline of a lake and the shorelines around an island act like the outside of an ice-cube tray. Ice comes up, and when it comes up to a certain point, it pushes against the surface and forms a ridge. In the middle of a lake, this ridge can stand up anywhere from two inches to six feet high. Every year that the lake freezes, local people can predict where these pressure ridges usually occur. An ice ridge can be in the same place year after year, then all of a sudden, it is in a different line, and you have to watch for it carefully if you are planning to a sail on a smooth surface.

This year was no different. Seven to nine inches of ice were not enough to form a pressure ridge and none was in sight yet. They would not have to worry about sailing along in their ice boats at sixty or ninety miles an hour and hitting a pressure ridge six inches high or two-feet high and the devastation that it could bring.

Harold and Bruce pulled down Concession Seventeen in Harvey Township and offloaded their ice boats. This was the same Concession that Curve Lake Indians used for parking and ice fishing out-of-season. Ice fishing was not allowed on the lake in the sixties, but local members of the reserve continued their history when and where their ancestors before them hunted and fished. The same spot the same lake had been fished for generations.

Harold and Bruce were ice sailors who wanted to avoid any Native ice fishermen and any of the garbage that some fishermen left behind on the ice. Catching an empty bait box, paper, liquor, or beer bottle under their ice skates could cause a loss of control and an upset. Fishermen usually waited a week or two until the ice was thicker and safer, so an early winter freeze-up was a time when the two friends knew the back channel would be free and clear for sailing.

A cold north wind, predicted by the local weather forecast, swept down the ice. The wind picked up and the sailors headed downwind towards Omemee. The ice was black and smooth, the best of the best. They both tacked upwind and moved up the west side of Boyd Island, close to the mouth of Bald Lakes. They stopped briefly on the north shore of Pigeon, near a rock shoal, and decided that they had enough wind and daylight time to sail down to the south weed beds of Pigeon and still make it back before dark, almost a twenty-mile ride. The fast route with the wind, down the east side of Boyd, would save time and give them a buffer before they lost the light.

The back channel funnelled wind. They could pick up speed there and then shoot out into the main part of the lake. They only had to negotiate one rock shoal in mid-channel and the rest was clear sailing.

They did not know that Joe Longfoot had been sent out by his mother to get fresh pickerel, the fish also called walleye. Joe continued his family's tradition of setting up fishing holes in mid-channel, just south of Concession Seventeen. He parked his truck beside the other two cars and trailers and carried his equipment, food, and drinks out onto the ice. After drilling three holes and setting his tip ups, he waited for a strike. He sat on his stool, a bait box, with his back to the north wind, waiting for the tip ups to move. Deep in thought and sipping on his flask of whisky, he was warm and comfortable. He knew that if he was patient but quick, fresh fish would be on his mother's dinner table, and all the family would be happy.

What Joe did not know was that two ice boats, upwind from him, were about to run him over at sixty miles per hour.

With luck, any person who gets run over on the ice ends up in the bone ward at the local hospital. Usually, however, he is killed instantly from head trauma or he bleeds to death from cuts.

Harold and Bruce flew down the back channel, tacking east and west, catching as much backwind as possible, keeping two skates on the ice, or three when needed. Joe, sitting on black ice, with his back to the wind, was wearing dark clothing that blended into the colours of the shoreline. He was not visible. In black ice conditions, there is no need to pull a white sheet over you as camouflage from patrolling aircraft. The wind whistled past Joe's hooded parka and his mind drifted to faraway places. He did not pick up the sound of the quickly-approaching ice skates.

It was all over in a split second. When he saw Joe sitting on his fishing stool, Harold dropped down on his third skate. He thought he saw Joe turn at the last moment but was not sure. Joe, seeing the ice boat heading towards him, only had time and sense of mind to lift his feet. Harold's right, outside skate took the box out from under Joe and swept the ice clear. The ice auger, bait box, flask, and the extra pair of gloves were gone. Everything below Joe's seat was swept away and he landed on the ice with nothing but his life.

Quickly, Harold and Bruce brought their boats under control and headed back upwind towards Joe. Joe rose slowly to his feet and watched as the two boats came closer.

None of the three men spoke. They all knew that their lives could have been swept away in a flash. Bruce finally broke the tension and said, "Joe that's one hell of a way to tap a friend on the shoulder." They all laughed. Joe declined a ride back to shore. He needed time to collect his thoughts. His mother would be furious that he did not have fresh fish for the evening meal. Harold replaced the flask as he knew Bruce had given an identical flask to his fishing buddy, Joe, and they often had a swallow together after a cold day fishing.

Soon after this event, Bruce's younger brother set up an ice hut rental business on Pigeon Lake. Renting ice houses to local First Nation's people for a percentage of their catch would supply his family with fresh fish all winter long. Local government officials were in a quandary over this business arrangement, as no money changed hands and no contracts, beside verbal ones, were given. Fishing gangs were happy, as they were much more comfortable out of the wind and snow, and a percentage of the catch seemed a fair trade. This historic barter system had no taxes.

Bruce and Ruthie were in love and were one of those couples that continued to be in love all their lives. They both had a natural talent for singing and enjoyed harmonizing together. No one else in their families was musical. At first, standing around a piano or organ was a foreign concept to both of them. They decided to try out for the church choir and were welcomed into this constantly-diminishing group.

The average age of remaining choir members was twice theirs, so they were often treated like children. Rehearsals on Wednesday nights and singing at church on Sunday mornings were fun. Children going to Sunday School were picked up and taken to church, while choir members were busy in the back room rehearsing songs for the service. Sunday school at nine-thirty and church at ten gave other parents time to clean the house or time to do other things for themselves without children interrupting.

Ruthie had ideas about what to do after choir on Sundays. She would undress Bruce in the car on the way from the church. Pulling into the garage, the two of them created enough heat that their car could be turned off on the coldest of days. Into their sixties and seventies, Ruthie would continue to surprise Bruce. Groceries could always be unpacked later and Christmas presents could be taken into the house, when they were remembered.

One day on arriving home and pulling into the garage, they were greeted by a gang of friends who had set up a surprise birthday party for Bruce. Ruthie dove to the floor of the car and put on Bruce's underwear and pants. She pulled her choir gown on top before the crowd descended on the car. Later, they had a good laugh, because she was wearing Bruce's underwear backwards from the rush to get dressed. It was a good thing that it was summertime as less clothing did not draw the same attention.

Summer Jobs

Bruce took two burlap bags, each the one-hundred-pound size, and filled them with the innards and head of a steer that the neighbours had butchered. He put two large rocks in the bottom of the bag and wired the top shut with strong fencing wire. In the Trent River near the town of Trent River, he carefully selected a spot where he had previously caught mud cat. He dropped the bag and noted three landmarks that would later line him up with the bags. Anytime you want to catch mud cat, you drop a worm bob, no hooks required, and lift the fish directly into a pail in your boat. Since mud cats are bottom feeders, they would start sucking at the two bags that Bruce dropped and would be easy to catch.

One spring day before March break, the job hunting holiday, a teacher at NDHS, Mr. Jack Richardson, told Bruce's class about a summer job he had when going to university. A Peterborough meat packer had an abattoir and meat-processing plant on George Street, exactly where the Holiday Inn Hotel is located today. Students working there had a summer job and were well-paid. Jack Richardson worked the night shift with his buddy and for fun they ran the picket-fence game. To play, kids take a stick and quickly pull it along any picket fence, dreaming that the sounds they make are from a musical instrument like a xylophone. During their meal break on the night shift, Jack and his friend played a different version of the picket-fence game in the cold room. In the cold room, beef and pork carcasses were hung on hooks from the ceiling track. Taking turns, the first person into the room would flick on the lights and, starting on the left, would run along the row of carcasses with a broom handle. The buddy would follow with a shovel and kill as many rats as possible, as they dropped out of the carcasses and tried to scurry away. When they had run all the rows of meat, the boys stopped to count dead and dying rats and kept score. Boy, did this game ever help with hand-eye coordination. Dead rats were shovelled out into Little Lake behind the plant.

At this time, the processing plant dumped all of its waste blood and animal parts directly into Little Lake. This kept the turtle, sucker, and mud cat population in that lake strong and healthy. That is why you located on a lake and that is what lakes are for. Years later, when the plant was torn down, people saw huge rats leaving the site and moving to other places in town. The plant was missed when it moved out of town. One lakeside resident that was instrumental in cleaning up Little Lake, summed it up when talking to her neighbour, "Because you did it in the past does not give you the right to do it in the future."

Many students scrambled to find a summer job. Prime jobs at General Electric, Outboard Marine, De Laval, Quaker Oats, Westclox, and Ovaltine in Peterborough often went to employees' sons or daughters. These branch plants of the multinationals provided the jobs that paid the most.

Rose's dad knew the owner of the local gravel pit in Westwood, who was interested, maybe talked into, hiring Rose to be a flag man. When the asphalt mixer and crusher were in the pit, trucks came and went every five minutes or more often. The owner needed a flag man in the quarry to help sort out the truckers as they headed for stock piles or the asphalt plant. In the quarry, the owner's trucks were busy filling the bins on the hill that fed the asphalt plant or were hauling pit run and rubble to the crusher. Outside trucks picked up asphalt, gravel, or pit run. Sometimes local farmers or neighbours came in with small trailers and trucks to pick up a yard or two. These smaller vehicles were in the way most of the time, but it was important to the owner to keep up good relations with everyone around his business.

Rose was hired to flag trucks at the intersection inside the entrance to the pit and to keep them moving, so they didn't have to stop or get bunched up at the weigh scales. Rose got Everett a job filling in for the men when they took their week's summer holidays. One week Everett might be in the tiny shack at the weigh scales, and on another, he would be driving a truck that filled bins for the asphalt plant and so on, until the summer was over.

Rose was a quick study and loved her job. The first day she memorized all the in-house equipment and most of the incoming trucks. She could spot the oily backs of dump trucks hauling asphalt, because drivers often sprayed too much diesel oil into the truck beds and this oil leaked out over the back flaps and tail gate. Diesel oil helps asphalt slide out of the truck easier. Drivers, who sprayed in too much oil, got yelled at by the yard boss and the operator on the asphalt spreader. Diesel oil made the road surface soft, and road inspectors made contractors rip out sections of new asphalt with too much oil in it and repair it before the roller packed the mixture. Asphalt spreaders were made by Barber Greene and, consequently, drivers often got nick-named Barbara. After a few weeks on the job, Rose was the boss for all the drivers in and out of the pit. If anyone tried to jump their turn, Rose would hold them back. A driver would only try that once. Some drivers were paid per trip, and the more trips per day, the more pay Friday night.

Rose watched how the trucks were loaded at the gravel stockpile and how the loader picked up the buckets of gravel to load a truck. With the sweep hand on her stopwatch, she determined how much time it took to load each truck. That seemed to differ, depending on where and how trucks backed into the pile. She then calculated the ideal time by determining the angle a truck should be on and the motion the loader should make to fill trucks the fastest. Asphalt trucks had the pit to themselves, when the others went home, and many days they would run until dark on the paving road. Bins feeding the asphalt plant had to be left full at the end of the day. In the morning the loader and gravel trucks would be working before anyone else came to the pit.

At home that first weekend, Rose took out a piece of graph paper and, with the measurements she had taken of the trucks, the loader, and the turning radius of the loaders, she determined the most efficient way to load trucks. Loaders, like most vehicles, have a tighter turning-circle in reverse than in forward. Articulated loaders, which pivot in the centre, have the same turning-circle forward and in reverse. She knew how many buckets were required per ton and how many bucket loads were required to fill each truck.

The single-axle trucks were much smaller than the new ones with double axles.

After work on Monday, she decided to take a big risk and show her work to the pit owner. She had shown diagrams and notes to her father and mother on the weekend and asked her dad how she should approach Cal. Her dad's best advice was to talk to Cal after work and shoot straight from the hip. "Don't waste time and get to the point quickly. If he hears the words, 'making more money' or 'saving money', you will have his attention instantly."

Rose did not know that her dad would call Cal on Sunday to prepare him for Rose's surprise visit.

On Monday after work at six o'clock, Rose went into the tiny office at the side of the pit. Cal was there behind his desk piled high with paper, two bearings from the conveyor that connected the sand and gravel bins to the asphalt plant, and a phone in one hand. She caught his eye and Cal motioned for her to sit down. Cal was one of those men who could not speak a sentence without at least four swear words. Good preachers practice for years to have a voice that flows so that words slide off their tongues as if they are sitting on the knees of God. Talking came naturally to Cal. He could describe a truck, a gear, a person, or anything else in life with an appropriate string of profanities so embedded in his chatter that you had to admire his command of the English language. His language was as colourful as he was, and he lived life to the fullest.

"Rose, what can I do for you?" Rose knew that someone must have spoken to Cal before she arrived, as she never before heard him utter a single sentence without punctuating it with profanities.

"Mr. Gordon, I can save you money and this chart will show you how and how much."

Cal looked at Rose over his dusty glasses, and said, "For Christ's sake, Rose, it's Cal."

Rose sketched out the path of the loader and indicated where the trucks should be positioned. She showed him the time it took to load each kind of truck, where the second and third truck should be waiting, the distance the loader travelled, the amount of fuel used, and the cost of fuel per day. She had also worked in the view of the driver in the truck, the view of the loader operator, and the reduction in the cost of repairing broken side boards, if drivers loaded in a different way. Cal sat quietly. He could not believe his eyes and ears as Rose laid out her new loading procedure. Small things add up and the savings per day, per week, per month were huge. Cal knew he was talking to a unique talent.

Cal looked over his glasses again, this time with a wink. "How do we get those dumb … son … to bloody well get their … in gear to change … ways."

Rose only heard him say "we" and "put this into place."

Rose knew the loader operators and, to a man, they would be motivated by beer. Cal always had a drop-in barbeque on Saturdays at the quarry. Everyone was invited and drivers, employees, neighbours, and customers would drop in with a six-pack and something to throw on the barbeque. Rose suggested that the three loader operators have a chance to see who could load a double-axle truck the fastest. First prize would be three cases of beer; second prize, two cases of beer; last place, one case of beer.

Cal had been born on a machine and could operate any piece of equipment. The story told was that Cal could fix machines on the run too. Cal would practise the procedure Rose laid out, and he would challenge his loader operators when they were finished their contest.

When the day arrived and two barbeques were getting fired up Cal dropped the idea of a contest on the three loader operators. They were on board right away, because, even if they lost, they would still go home with a case of beer. Six cases of beer stacked up was a mouth-watering sight.

Before they started, the drivers all agreed what a full truck should look like. The three drivers took turns. Their times were only a few seconds apart. When loading a double-axle, their longest and shortest times were only one minute and two seconds apart.

When they were finished, Cal said, "I think I can f… well do better than that, and you know how I hate to show off. Guys, if I can't beat your times, I will double your cases."

The three loader operators knew that they could find room for more beer in their trucks.

Cal jumped on an articulated loader, headed for the pile of gravel, and told the driver exactly where to back up and park. The flag dropped and the stopwatch was punched. When his truck was loaded, the time was twenty seconds faster than the best previous time posted.

Cal's reputation went up another notch.

The extra cases of beer were soon gone.

Rose's new way of loading became standard procedure at the pit. After this change, Cal asked Rose to look at all the other operations in the quarry. This time she was able to bring in Ruthie's boyfriend, Bruce, to take over her flagging position.

Meanwhile, as old loaders wore out, they were replaced with new articulating loaders, which had buckets with larger capacities. A truck that had to wait to be loaded meant lost business. A driver would go to the pit that was closest and that could load him the fastest. Contractors, landscapers, and builders all relied on their trucks to get in and get out as quickly as possible, as every load cost time and thus money, and the closer the pit was to a worksite, the better a job could be priced. Rose knew that if she could get trucks into the pit and out as quickly as possible, she could undercut the times of two closer quarries.

Moving the weigh scale that all trucks had to run over to get out of the pit was another strategic decision. Rose watched and listened as drivers changed gears. Then she determined the best location for the scales, not only to prevent trucks from having to shift and downshift before they got to the stop sign at the road, but also to smooth out the flow of traffic moving out of the pit. This would save seconds on each trip.

Rose also noticed that most truckers bought a coffee and snack, usually a doughnut, to begin their day. Most trucks made their first trip to the quarry between 6 and 8 a.m. Snacks for morning breaks, lunches, and afternoon breaks were often eaten on the run. Could the weigh scale operator pass out a coffee and doughnut to the driver as he or she handed out the weigh slip? Two big coffee urns could provide enough coffee for two hours, if one was started early and the other turned on at seven. To provide the doughnuts, she thought of her neighbour, Mary Miles, who had five children on the farm and had just lost her husband in a farming accident. The tractor he was operating to pull out a stone in his hayfield upended and fell backwards, rolling on him, and crushing him in front of his oldest son. This was in the days before roll bars and seat belts became standard equipment on tractors. Mary was always looking for ways to make ends meet and the opportunity to provide bake goods sounded too good to be true. Before long, truckers were getting their morning coffee, and not only doughnuts, but also muffins, butter tarts, and other pastries at the pit. Each day there was a choice between the standard fare and something new. Most truckers knew about Mary's situation and were happy to buy breakfast and snacks at the weigh station. To save time making change, the cost of coffee and a snack was one dollar and the driver chose the snack. As a driver reached out to get the weigh slip, he got a cup of hot coffee and his snack too. When drivers made the decision on which pit to draw from, most of them came back to this one.

This plan was so successful that Mary was offered the weigh scales job as well and she accepted. Her family needed a cash income to pay the mortgage and stay on the farm.

Mary watched carefully to see which brand of cigarettes and cigars each of the guys smoked. She always seemed to have a spare package on hand to lend out. The men would be back the next day to replace that pack, as they appreciated getting their smoke fix when they needed it.

Mary always kept Cal's cigars on hand, as he seemed to be running out of them more often these days. Keep the boss happy.

One day Cal dropped in to talk to Mary and she could see he had something troubling on his mind. Cal, the tough guy, wore everything on his sleeve. "Mary, I have a question for you."

Mary did not know what to expect.

"You are selling pop to the truckers and they are leaving bottles all over the pit."

Mary's heart sank. She needed this job. The extra income from her sales was putting clothes on her kids' backs.

"Do you think that this Sunday afternoon your kids could come to the pit and help pick up bottles? I will have the half-ton truck empty and your oldest and I can return the bottles on Monday. You would be doing me a favour."

Mary's mind was racing for an answer, as she did not expect that question, and certainly not an opportunity for her children. "Sure," she sputtered. "What would be a good time?"

She didn't hear the answer.

The next day, Mary told Rose what Cal had said and was quite surprised when Rose said, "I will be here to help too."

Sunday after lunch, the whole family arrived at the pit. Rose had gone earlier with piles of boxes, as high as the roof of the cab, tied down in the back. Everett would be there later too.

Mitch Miles, the oldest son, was reluctant. He was in a constant state of sorrow, and when he wasn't thinking about his dad, he was concerned about all the farm chores. Mitch wasn't asked to fill his dad's shoes, he just assumed that position.

His young shoulders drooped with all of his responsibilities. Neighbours and near-by farmers helped out as much as they could.

"Mitch," called Rose. "Who should I take in the truck to unload the boxes? There isn't much room in the cab."

"Annie, go with Rose."

"Hey Annie, let's get the ropes off the boxes and make a place in the back for you to stand. You can stand on the tailgate and pitch off the boxes as I drive around the pit."

Annie happily sat on the driver's side of the truck box ready to play bombs away.

The cardboard boxes were dropped, with appropriate sound effects, all over the pit, along the roads, close to the crusher and asphalt plant, and into every corner where empty bottles had been tossed.

Rose circled back to Mitch.

"Mitch, Annie needs help to load the full boxes onto the truck."

"Take Jordie, he needs a break."

Within two hours all the boxes were filled and collected. Cal's half-ton cab had just enough room left for one person to slide in. The box and trailer behind were both filled to capacity.

Cal had his Saturday barbeque out, fired up and ready to go. There was cold pop for the kids and cold white wine for the ladies. Cal's hands were cupped comfortably around a beer.

The money collected from these empties bought all the text books and supplies required for Mary's children to go back to school, and new pairs of shoes for three of the children. In the early fifties, elementary and secondary students had to provide their own text books. Passing down books, as well as clothes, happened in families first, then with relatives and neighbours. If used books could not be found, parents or students went to the Rexall Drug Store in town to purchase new texts. Elementary and high school students purchased their own books. For high school students, French and Latin books were given out for a dollar deposit. You would put your name in ink on the inside front cover under the last person's name. The list could be long. You got your money back, if books were returned in good shape.

Ruthie and Rose were best friends and they enjoyed being with each other. Ruthie's parents owned the wrecking yard on the outskirts of town. She had four brothers, all of whom were younger. She had to look after them. Ruthie, being the first child that could hang onto a cutting torch, learned the trade first and she was expected to teach the next in line.

Ruthie's dad knew that he was in competition with big wrecking yards in Peterborough and Cobourg and he had to make everything count. "We buy wrecks for parts and sell parts for wrecks" was the catchy way Jerry Nurse in Peterborough advertised, so his yard came to mind first when people were looking for parts.

With almost no advertising budget, how else do you compete and stay in business? Sell every part and waste nothing. When Ruthie was younger, she could crawl in and out of just about all the wrecked vehicles that came into the yard. Getting parts out and to the customer was difficult when doors, hoods and trunks would not open, which was the case if the vehicles had been jammed sidewise in roadside collisions. Ruthie learned all the tricks of opening and starting vehicles with a screwdriver or piece of copper wire. She was a natural and could climb into a side window, back window, or even through the trunk into a back seat and, in minutes, grab a roof lining without damaging a thing.

Ruthie was in charge of waste liquids and every vehicle that came into the yard to be wrecked had to have all tanks emptied. Most auto wreckers, at this time, did not empty tanks on a vehicle and liquids would end up leaking out and soiling the ground. At Ruthie's dad's yard, gasoline and diesel oil were stored in forty-five gallon drums. Brake fluid, radiator antifreeze, differential fluid, transmission fluid, and all other fluids were collected and sold. Ruthie learned to siphon before she learned how to suck on a cigarette. She only smoked for a few months and decided that she was not giving her time and money to a cigarette company. Not even Lloyd Robertson, smoking his du Maurier cigarettes on TV, could convince her it was a good thing to do.

Rose's ability to understand movement, flow, and space, from her time in the pit, resulted in a consulting business.

Everett was good with paperwork, phone conversations, and follow-up. Everett also saw things differently from Rose. After working at the same location, they were constantly surprised at the similarities and the differences they picked up in the daily operation of a company. Rose had a partner, they were a team.

Chapter Four

Ring The Bell, Stop The Line, Re-Tool

One day, they were on Highway 401, the major expressway running east and west in Ontario. Traffic was slow due to heavy rain. Everett was driving east heading for the #35, Highway 115 exit, when he noticed tractor trailers were passing him, one after the other. On a stretch between the Don Valley Parkway and Kennedy Road, the rain just poured down. Everett could hardly see the road in front of the car, yet these forty-ton rigs were whizzing by him. How could they see and he could not?

Then he saw it. He was sure he knew why truck drivers could see and he couldn't.

"Rose," he said, "I have to show you something when we get home." After they unpacked the car, he asked Rose to help him explain what had happened in the rain storm.

Everett parked the car in the driveway in front of the house with the windshield wipers running. He took the garden hose and stood back about fifteen feet and sprayed the windshield. He asked Rose to sit in the back seat and look out the driver's side. Then he asked Rose to sit behind the passenger's seat and look out that side of the windshield. Rose could not believe her eyes.

The passenger side windshield wiper swept water over into the driver's side and dumped it into the driver's line of vision. The passenger wiper cleaned the window with both forward and reverse strokes, leaving the passenger with the best view of the road ahead. Everett soon concluded that a driver is blinded with today's wiper system!

Rose went into the house, loaded new batteries into the VHS camera, and started filming a movie from the back seat of the car of the two views of the windshield being sprayed with water. The old expression: Back seat drivers may be right after all.

The next time it rained, Everett and Rose drove around looking for cars with wipers that were blinding drivers.

Out of nowhere, Everett said, "I know why your Uncle Jim pulled in front of that tractor trailer."

When Rose was in her thirties, her Uncle Jim and his family were killed driving to their sons' hockey game the second week of December, on a Friday night.

It was one of those early storms when the snow falls in big flakes, wet and sticky. The road was slippery and the snow piled up on everything. Uncle Jim was turning left off Highway # 7 into the parking lot at the hockey arena when a tractor trailer loaded with pulp wood logs hit them broadside.

Jim and his wife Grace, their two sons Dan and Bert, and the boys' hockey buddy Fred, were killed instantly. The van was crushed like a tin can. The transport truck carried the van down the road into a ditch and pinned and flattened it against a large elm tree. The police investigation cleared the truck driver. Another driver, behind Jim that night, saw Jim's van pull across the lane towards the arena right in front of the tractor trailer.

The van was towed away by the local town wrecker, and a number of people from town went to inspect the wreckage. This one would be packed for the steel mill; there were no useable parts to sell.

Looking at any wreck that has taken one's life is like visiting at the funeral home to make sure it has really happened. In this case, five lives were lost. Wreckers take killing cars to the very back of their lots out of sight on the day of the funeral.

Rose knew that her uncle liked to drink rye and coke but he never touched a drop until after a game when he was home safe and sound. He was an excellent driver, did not speed, and never got into fender benders. He was always so careful. She wondered why he would pull in front of a tractor trailer on a slippery road.

Uncle Jim's van had one of those long sweeping windshields that gave anyone in the car the feeling of being in the cockpit of an airplane. The driver's side wiper must have piled up snow against the left windshield pillar and that pillar would have grown wider as snow accumulated. The left windshield pillar, with snow, ice or mud pushed up against it, forms a visual block for the driver not the passenger. On a curve that bends to the driver's left, an approaching truck or car can be visually blocked from the driver, who assumes that the lane is clear, and makes a left turn into a road, driveway, or right into an oncoming vehicle.

The hockey rink that Uncle Jim was heading for was located on the left side of a road with a long, sweeping, left curve. That night in the wet snow, an oncoming tractor trailer would have been blocked from view by that left pillar on the windshield made larger and wider with wet sticky snow.

Imagine Uncle Jim turning left into the arena, blinded on the left by that large pillar of snow and Grace, on the passenger side, seeing the truck clearly.

Her scream would never be heard again.

Uncle Jim's van had been crushed long ago, but there were still plenty of models of the same van on the road. Ruthie found them one in the wrecking yard. Rose recreated the accident scene with it. The head position in the seat, the pillar with snow build-up, and the area to the left where the pillar blocks were all calculations she carefully graphed out on paper. They included distances to the left and right and projections in front of the van.

The next Saturday, they would take their notes and the van complete with wrecker plates that Ruthie lent them, and visit the site where her uncle's family had been killed. They would do their first test during the daytime, with the sun out, and with perfect weather conditions. This was not a trip that they would enjoy, but they could hardly wait to get going.

They drove at the speed that they thought her uncle might have driven that night in snowy conditions. They drove by the arena entrance, turned around, and drove back. They did this twice, each taking turns driving, without saying anything to each other. This is the way they worked during the week, each sensing a situation, both taking mental notes of what they saw and how they felt.

On the fourth trip, Rose pulled over onto the right shoulder and stopped the van in the position that would show the exact line of vision her Uncle had when he turned left into the driveway of the arena. In her hand, Rose held strips of white Bristol board that she had measured, starting with a one-inch wide strip and going up to a five-inch strip. All the strips were about as high as the windshield. Starting by taping the one-inch strip to the left pillar, Rose measured the driver's line of vision. She continued until all five strips had been taped to the window and the line of measurement taken. She and Everett concluded that, if the snow build-up on the left pillar was two inches or more, there was no way a driver could have seen the transport truck. The tractor trailer would have been completely hidden behind the left pillar.

The next question was why did Uncle Jim not see the headlights of the oncoming truck? They could only speculate about this until they could test their theory in snowfall and at night. In a wet snow, headlights get coated with snow and a mixture of road salt, sand, and slush thrown up by vehicles driving ahead of them. The headlights of the transport truck would have been dimmed by this road grunge and the wet snow. They also noticed that two of the arena parking lot lights were placed close to the driveway into the arena. The sideways glare of the parking lot lights might have lit up the falling snow just enough that, in effect, a white blind went across the road.

Rose and Everett waited anxiously for winter and a night snowstorm to check out their theories. They missed the first two night storms but, for the third one in December, they were both at home. The forecast called for wet snow.

They phoned Ruthie and said, "Pull out the van. We are on our way." There was no way Ruthie and Bruce were not going on this double date.

They got to the arena, pulled over onto the right shoulder, and looked in amazement as the arena lights lit up the snow and formed a white curtain on the road. With the build-up of snow on the pillar by the driver's side windshield wiper, they could see that no driver would have seen a transport truck or any other on-coming vehicle until the last one-hundred feet. At sixty miles per hour, a vehicle is moving at eighty-eight feet per second and once a driver commits to making a turn, he cannot change his mind. Rose and Everett concluded that if Uncle Jim had seen the truck, he would not have turned left into the arena. Uncle Jim did not see the truck, but his wife Grace probably did, and she could do nothing after the turn was started. The speed of the truck would not have been sixty but once it T boned the van it would not be able to stop in slippery conditions and the slide into the elm tree was inevitable.

Rose and Everett knew they had discovered a real problem for the car industry. They wondered what their next step ought to be.

How could they tell some of the largest and richest companies in the world that they have designed vehicles that are killing their customers? How could they, as ordinary people, deal with car companies with bottomless budgets for lawyers and the reputation for stealing patents, and grinding people down in the courtrooms with legal expenses?

They developed a plan. First, they had to do some homework and check out which models of cars had this wiper design flaw.

They concluded that any situation in which you have to use your windshield wipers, the passenger side wiper sweeps the water in front of the driver. Depending on how much rain is falling, the pool of water pushed in front of the driver can be inches wide. There is no question that driving with your wipers on is dangerous.

What Rose and Everett did not realize, was that they were in a situation that is best described as a modern version of "The Emperor Has No Clothes." Millions of drivers are unaware that they can be blinded by the wiper system in their vehicles.

They decided to check right-hand-drive cars to see how those wiper systems worked. Sure enough, all right-hand-drive cars and light trucks had the same problem. This time the passenger wiper on the left side sweeps rain in front of the driver on the right, making right turns, in rainy or snowy conditions, dangerous. The driver's vision was compromised in these cars too.

All two-wiper systems, in cars or light trucks worked the same way. The passenger wiper threw water or snow in front of the driver. On many models the passengers wiper stopped directly in front of the driver.

The only systems in which wipers did not dump rain in front of the driver were the one-wiper system and the double-sweep system; however, one of these still piled up snow on the driver's left post. As well, these two alternate systems were both expensive and prone to costly repairs and appeared to only be available on a few select models.

Next, they pondered on the idea of patenting a solution themselves. This meant trying to sell their patent to car companies and large part suppliers that were notorious for taking advantage of any small inventor. Rose's other main concern was the reputation of these powerful companies for stealing patents. Her conscience also reminded her that people's lives were in danger. The demise of her own Uncle Jim's family strengthened her conviction to look at their bank books very carefully. As Rose and Everett were evaluating their willingness and level of commitment Everett drew an analogy to following a drunk driver. Do you simply follow at a safe distance or do you report it. Rose knew in her heart…they closed their bank book and decided to patent the solution.

In reviewing existing patents, they saw that no one had a patent on their new system. Under patent laws, there were certain criteria that they would have to meet, before a new patent was given. A new patent would last for seventeen years, and they would have to defend their patent against anyone who tried to infringe on it or use it illegally. The two young entrepreneurs decided to use a large downtown law firm in Toronto to do the formal patent search and to apply for a new patent.

Rose drafted and sent a letter to the Canadian President of the worlds' largest car company, and a phone call a few days later directed them to make an appointment with the Manager of Research and Development and New Business Ventures. They definitely had the correct person to call.

A call to General Motors in Oshawa, Canada, was well-received and an appointment to come and show their idea was extended. Everett explained that he had a VHS video tape to show and, if the company could have a VCR and TV set up ahead of time, it would take less time to explain.

Rose and Everett drove to Oshawa and parked in the visitor's parking lot. GMC vehicles surrounded their non-GMC truck. Inside, reception was businesslike and professional and a new Buick convertible was on display in the foyer. They were quickly ushered up to the third floor, where they met Mr. Post for the first time. He was busy, but welcomed them to sit down, and offered them a cup of coffee. They declined as they were anxious to show their video and then to talk further. Mr. Post did not have the VHS player and TV equipment set up and seemed reluctant to do so. Everett explained that it had been requested ahead of time. There was a moment of silence then he called his secretary to set up a room for a video presentation. After four or five minutes of chit chat, the secretary buzzed Mr. Post, and said the room was ready.

Walking down to the room past many offices, they were observed by people taking time from their busy work to glance up and see who was moving in the corridors of bureaucracy.

Once in the conference room, Everett loaded his tape and the five-minute video was on. Rose watched Mr. Post. Everett caught the drama out of the corner of his eye. Clearly, the film showed water from the passenger's wiper being dumped in front of the driver, obscuring his vision until the driver's wiper swept down to clear the windshield. This happened over and over again. Mr. Post reacted. "I can't believe what I'm seeing." Then regaining his corporate composure, he said, "In some conditions, pre-arranged, this might happen."

Everett and Rose left a copy of the master tape with him to show to GMC decision-makers in Detroit. Mr. Post had already told them that decisions are not made in Canada.

Their next appointment was with Ford Canada and the company's Chief Corporate Lawyer. Time and date were set up and the procedure was similar to GMC's. In the Ford situation, the lawyer was on time and prepared. Rose and Everett were welcomed into the board room where the equipment to show VHS tapes was set up. After watching the tape, the lawyer said, "This is really important. I want to show this to our engineering department." Everett and Rose knew that statement was the "kiss of death", as the engineers would not likely admit that an outsider could have an idea better than an engineered-based idea. After all, engineers were paid professionals.

The third meeting was with a director of Volvo Canada at his home in Aurora, Ontario. He had a VCR set up and was anxious to see the tape immediately. At the end of the viewing he said, "Let's go outside. I have two cars in the laneway and I have to see this for myself." He started one Volvo after the other and sprayed their windshields to see how the wipers worked in the rain. Then he exclaimed, "I now understand why I could not see during a rain storm in Florida, when we were travelling there last week. Our company is so committed to safety that we will immediately change our wiper system."

Everett and Rose were not so lucky getting appointments with wiper manufacturers. All attempts at getting an interview with any of the major wiper blade manufacturers resulted in "We will get back to you."

A call to both the Canadian and the American government agencies that regulate auto windshield standards ended in a standard response: "Car companies are meeting the standards that are set down on wiping the windshield clean." Everett tried to explain that car wipers did wipe, but that they also swept and piled water and snow in front of the driver. Never mind that the snow thickened the left pillar and was a visual barrier to seeing un-coming vehicles when executing a left turn. His explanation fell on deaf ears. Everett and Rose concluded that government agencies are only interested in the number of square inches that are being cleared. The idea that the driver should be able to see is not a concern or a criteria for windshield wipers.

One retired engineer from GMC told Everett that they would never be successful in getting their patent accepted because of the liability issue with car companies. In his words: "Once the general population is aware that the driver's vision is blocked during rain or snow, they will demand a retrofit, and the cost to refit millions and millions of light trucks and cars will be astronomical. If companies install a new system on any future cars, it will also alert the population that the old system has a problem triggering a staggering recall. Forget it until you have the resources to win this battle."

Rose and Everett began to feel that time and money were lacking as other life matters had been put on hold in order to pursue their conviction. They predicted that someday a law firm would assign a junior clerk to file a class action suit against car companies. Rose said to Everett, "Uncle Jim is watching from above. He probably has just scraped off the snow for the kids to play shinny on the Mill Pond. He has lots of time and "<u>don't</u>" need the money." They both laughed and Everett laughed the loudest as he sensed Rose was putting it behind her and everyone missed her wacky sense of humour.

A couple of weeks later Manley and his wife Cora were over for Sunday dinner at Rose's parents' place in Westwood. After dinner around the big table Rose decided to ask Manley his views about the stonewalled rejection of their idea from the auto companies and government agencies. After showing the video, Manley was very careful with his answer, as he had seen similar situations many times himself. He thought out loud. "Every working person has a job that provides an income for a family's necessities. People work in companies that have rules and regulations that reward and punish certain types of behaviour. These rules often have no correlation to what the company must say and print for the public to hear and digest."

"Every person remembers the term, Mr. WIFM, a What's-in-It-For-Me? Will I keep my job? Will this help me get ahead? Do I have the time to get involved? Will a problem disappear if I do nothing?"

"From what you have told me the people you have met with have no interest in your idea as they will not personally benefit from it. The bureaucracy they live in will not reward them, but in fact will likely punish them for promoting your patent."

Manley's advice; "the only way you will be successful with your idea is to convince the public and the car drivers of the world that there is a problem. Only their collective voices will change the situation."

Manley then predicted, "The day will come when you will negotiate a settlement for your patent. The cost of ignoring the situation is too great."

"Be patient. If car companies ever said that they knew what they were doing, then they would be admitting liability for many past accidents and deaths. The associated costs and the cost to retrofit millions of vehicles that are on the road today might put them into chapter eleven. If, however, they said that they did not know about the problem, then your patent would be sound. The industry would be at your door to negotiate."

"Government agencies that have approved past windshield wiper applications are in the same boat. If they say they knew there was a problem, then they can be sued along with car companies. If they come out and say that your patent is a new invention and a much-needed improvement, then you have the backing of all governments in all the countries that manufacture cars and light trucks."

"You will get your day in court. If the industry is smart, they will negotiate, but their track record is ugly."

Then Manley said something that startled them both. "It's the Golden Rule: Whoever holds the gold makes the rules."

"In your case it is the insurance companies, and many of these are owned by banks. Insurance companies will not want to be taken to court to pay out huge claims. Class action suits will be filed against every manufacturer and the settlement will be huge. Imagine anyone in Norwood that new Jim and Grace and the boys, sitting on the jury. Just about every Judge in the world drives a car. Every small town has their own story to tell. I predict that the insurance companies will give each policy holder a short time period to retrofit, and then they will cancel a consumer's insurance policy if that person does not comply. There are probably seven-hundred million vehicles that will need to be fixed. This will be the largest recall in history. No one in the world has ever stopped all the production lines at one time. This will be the first." The insurance industry, not the government, will stop the production lines around the world. They will just come out and say we will not insure any new vehicle unless the windshield wiper system is changed so the driver can see clearly when it rains or snows.

"Have you decided on the law firm to represent you when the auto industry comes calling?"

Rose and Everett heard Manley very clearly but did not completely understand the profound impact of the meaning of corporate life. They also were not quite sure how large seven-hundred million was.

Rose and Everett were still in the belief that the invention of a better mouse trap would be recognized and purchased by the public.

Cora sat quietly knitting through the entire conversation. She added, I have just finished my second reading of the book, "For Whom The Bell Tolls." By Ernest Hemingway. Don't they stop the assembly lines with a bell?"

Cora turned to Rose, "Rose, your major was English, I hope you are keeping notes as this venture in your business and life would make an excellent chapter eleven." Everyone laughed but Rose's dad, Clint only smiled as he was remembering once again his son Jake and how much he would have enjoyed hearing his sister.

Epilogue

Today's courier companies and delivery service businesses often plan their routes to minimize left turns. Statistics show that turning left in the rain or snow or simply just driving in rain or snow causes highway collisions. Over seventeen percent of fatalities are directly related to left turns. Many of these collisions are not accidents at all. Our so-called "killer highways" are filled with vehicles equipped with faulty windshield wiper systems. Those are not accidents.

Chapter Five

The Brothers and the Bottle Trade

Many small communities in Ontario have no beer store or liquor store in their town limits, as the Prohibition Movement of the thirties did its job and dried up towns. The Temperance Movement was a strong and successful force. When a town is dry, it means that alcoholic beverages cannot be sold in a retail store, restaurant, hotel, or any other piece of real estate. This makes for a "bootlegger's heaven", as the population still wants the product, but has to drive for a distance to a wet town. Wet means that alcoholic sales are permitted, provided that the rules of the Alcohol and Gaming Commission of Ontario are followed.

Norwood had two bootleggers in the early sixties and they did a thriving business. They sold to anyone they knew, or to you, if they knew your parents. At sixteen, if you were old enough to drive a car and could get it down the laneway, you could buy anything you wanted. Anyone who could not handle booze was placed on The List. Many names came on and off the list but the one thing that remained was once your name was on it, you could not beg, borrow or buy a drink of any kind.

When local politicians became too tipsy to drive after an outing, they were given a free ride home by the police. One officer would drive the member-in-good-standing home, and the other officer would drive the politician's car. This was the Ride Program of the early fifties. People who ran for political office were respected and protected by their communities. Inebriated politicians were quietly tucked into bed and were back on the job the next day helping out their constituents.

Making your own moonshine was very common in Norwood, and family recipes would be carefully guarded and passed only between relatives. When you saw someone picking up a bottle of liquor and turning it upside down a couple of times, you knew you were looking at a moonshine drinker. By turning the bottle, its contents were mixed, so that the risk of having a full shot of contaminated killer was reduced. If a moonshine batch was run too long, so-called poison collected and mixing it up reduced its effect. Since the moonshine had nearly one-hundred percent alcohol, a person having a drink cut the volume and took only a small portion of this liquor at a time or they would be under the table immediately.

Distilling during a windy period or a storm reduced chances that the bootlegger would be caught. A cold winter day, when chimney smoke went straight up, was the safest time to work. Odours would not give them away. A year's supply of moonshine could be produced very quickly and at pennies a bottle. Few products were as profitable as illegal liquor.

In its earlier days, Norwood, a mainly Irish community, had a number of bars and places of libation. When Norwood went dry in the fifties, all the folks from Norwood had to drive six miles east to shop at beer or liquor stores in Havelock or drive six miles south to Hastings. The only way a beer store or liquor store could open in Norwood itself was to have the voted approval of the town. Every time the council brought the vote to the Norwood public, a majority would turn it down.

In Ontario, beer stores were and are still owned and operated by Brewers Retail. This consortium of major breweries owns and operates beer stores at the pleasure of AGCO, the Alcohol and Gaming Commission of Ontario, and you had better follow its rules and regulations. These rules and regulations determine the profit margins of beer companies. Over time, all large Canadian beer companies have been sold to foreign interests. *Canada has only a few small Canadian-owned and operated beer companies today. They must deal with the foreign owned Brewers Retail.*

This is where our story unfolds. We will be following Frank and his brother Rusty from being young boys into their careers in the spirit industry.

Rusty and Frank's parents, Arnold and Barbara, owned one of two small grocery stores in Norwood. In the early sixties, the idea of self-serve was a few years away. No store of any type was self-serve. Customers would come to the store or send their children with a handwritten list of items they needed. The store clerk would take the list and rewrite it on a piece of paper. As the clerk went around the store, he or she sourced all the goods and carried them back to the sales counter. The price of the item would be written down on the paper too, and at the end of the list, the clerk would total the amount. The store clerk would add the numbers up and then down to verify that the total was correct. None of the canned, glass, or bagged goods had an individual price marked on the container. Later on, prices were put on shelves, and then on individual goods. Frank loved using the pricing gun. He was quick and fast and dreamed of being a drummer. Errors made by inexperienced employees became the driving force behind the idea of self-service and other changes. Adding machines were to come later too.

Frank started working in the family store at seven years of age and he was needed. Rusty was already nine and pulling his weight. After closing at five o'clock, the family had supper and then went down to the store below to stock up for the next day. Frank was in charge of white and brown sugar, flour, salt, and molasses. The store received these items in bulk and Frank's dad, Arnold, would put the one-hundred pound bags in the corner of the back room beside the weigh scales. Using a scoop, Frank would fill two, five or ten-pound paper bags with flour, salt, or sugar. A string around each bag held the top closed. The weight was printed on each flour or sugar bag. The container of molasses in the back room would be put on its side on a wide shelf. Arnold showed his son how to open and turn the container of molasses and then fill clean bottles. The first two bottles were always the hardest to fill; after those, he had a bit of slack time to get the next bottle in place. Licking sticky fingers at the end was the tip for doing a good job. Frank made sure the shelves were filled, and then it was time to do his school work.

Frank considered himself lucky, as his buddies at school were from local farms where the routine was up at five-thirty, to the barn to do chores, change into school clothes, breakfast at seven-thirty, school bus at eight, school at eight forty-five. Home off the bus at four-thirty, change into work clothes, do the barn chores until six, then supper. In June you had to fit in haying, homework and exams. In the winter it was homework time after dinner. In the spring, it was calving time, and in the fall, harvest and fence-building after supper until dark. Then homework.

Saturdays were spent carrying out bags of groceries for customers. Frank kept an eye on the pre-measured goods and would slip away between customers and refill the shelves. He had responsibilities and enjoyed them. Being told twice how to do something was the worst punishment Frank could think of and he did everything to avoid that.

The one break Frank and Rusty had, were the two days a year they were allowed to take off work to collect bottles. The Monday and Tuesday of spring break in March was their time to have fun and make money. Snow, along the sides of the roads, was in melt-down and the litter and bottles of the winter were starting to poke up their heads. Collecting returnable bottles would continue Sunday afternoons until all the snow melted along the sides of the road.

When the boys were eleven and thirteen, they would ride out on their two-wheelers to collect bottles along Number Seven Highway towards Peterborough. Pop bottles and beer bottles were worth two cents each. Liquor bottles and wine bottles were not returnable then. Once you have taken time to dig a non-returnable bottle out of the mud or snow, you reach a point that you smash it so you won't make that mistake again. Frank and Rusty would take turns throwing a liquor bottle up in the air and then the other boy would try to hit it with another bottle. Scores were recorded. Two points if they both broke, one if just one bottle broke, and minus one if you missed entirely. Later on, a softball coach was amazed at Rusty's skill on third base. He could hit the first baseman's glove every time. No one on the team was as accurate or as quick as Rusty. Once they filled their two bags, the brothers would slip them onto their bicycle handle bars and head for home. In a few hours they could collect over twenty dollars in pop bottles and the same amount in beer bottles. Town folk that passed the boys on the highway collecting bottles knew for sure that Arnold and Barb were not making a fortune owning and operating a grocery store.

Rusty enjoyed teaching his younger brother and would try to answer any question. If he needed to, he could make up something that sounded reasonable.

"Rusty, why do people throw all these bottles onto the side of the road? They could turn them in and make money."

"Evidence, Frank. Think about it. You and your buddies are drinking and driving and you finish a beer or a last swig of whiskey. Are you going to leave the empties in the car for the police to find?" From an early age, Frank learned that when rules are made, they often have unexpected consequences.

One day, their father Arnold mentioned to the boys that Mr. Flet, the owner of the hardware store, was interested in acquiring some clean wine bottles.

Frank spoke first, "Why would he want clean wine bottles?"

"Not sure. You will have to ask."

On the way home from school, Frank dropped in to see Mr Flet. Mrs Flet was there and she told Frank that they needed a supply of clean bottles as they were running short. Linseed oil, turpentine, boiled oil, and various other products were shipped in forty-five gallon drums. These liquids were then bottled and labelled for customers.

She promised, "We will give you seven cents for every clean wine and liquor bottle like this one, but we must be able to see the contents inside." Frank realized he had smashed hundreds of those bottles, but would do so no more.

A market for other liquor bottles grew when Rusty discovered that moonshine makers also needed empty bottles. Frank, the budding entrepreneur, knew that the hardware store would buy new bottles for seven cents, but bootleggers did not want to be seen buying new bottles, as that might tip off the cops. One moonshine maker was covered, as his bottles were hidden under the guise of a maple syrup operation.

Rusty raised his price for empty wine and liquor bottles to six cents, and a number of friends in Havelock and Hastings joined his payroll, as bottle collectors. Drinking, driving and throwing bottles happened on every road.

Then, it seemed like overnight and his business went bust. Bulk sales of oils and turpentine to hardware stores were replaced with sales of products in pre-packaged containers. Also, one of the moonshine makers was aging and closing down his business to anyone outside of his family. The boys learned two other valuable lessons: markets turn on a dime and don't put all your eggs in one basket. There might be other markets for discarded bottles - maybe in maple syrup.

Cal, the pit owner from Westwood, was driving into town one day to pick up a conveyor belt that had been back-ordered. He recognized Frank and stopped on the side of the road. "Hey Frank, load those bottles into the back and I will drop them off at the store."

Cal was quick to recognize an opportunity for the two oldest children of Mary at the gravel pit to make some decent pocket money. Mary sold pop to truckers all summer long and with no place inside their trucks to put the empties, truck drivers just tossed them into the gravel pit. Trucks in the early sixties did not have air conditioning. Sitting on the side of the road with tons of hot asphalt behind your seat, waiting your turn to dump into the spreader was hot work, so you needed a cold pop to hit the spot.

From age seven to eleven, Frank's chores and responsibilities increased gradually, as his older brother Rusty moved up the line of command. From age twelve to fourteen, stocking shelves and perishable goods was added to Frank's list of duties. Store-closing and clean-up were shared responsibilities for everyone. Later, at age seventeen and eighteen, Frank would operate the complete business on his own for a week at a time, when his parents were called away to look after aging grandparents. Calling parents for help or advice was the last thing he wanted to do.

Hiring staff was fun, but with that responsibility came the firing that needed to be done from time to time. The rule was that you fired the staff that you hired. Theft and laziness were the major reasons for letting someone go. In a small town you never actually fired someone, as that person had to save face in the community. At the end of the process, the released employee always had some legitimate reason for not working at the store any longer.

Once inventory started to go missing, employee schedules would be changed and by putting together different combinations of employees, the boss could soon isolate the person responsible. The next step was to find out how this employee was moving goods out the door.

When it was Frank's turn to fire anyone, he followed his dad's method. Frank would strike up a conversation with the employee and in the following kibitzing would mention the items that were going missing and would solicit that employee's help in trying to stop the shortages. Sometimes this would stop the problem, but in most cases the theft would start up again. Frank would inform his dad or mom and they would be on standby when that employee was stopped outside the store.

Barbara was in charge of the cashiers and she had a number of systems in place to catch dishonest employees.

Customer theft started as soon as self-service began. Frank was thirteen when self-service was introduced. He soon became an expert at catching customers shoplifting.

One of the funniest thefts occurred when a middle-aged lady stole a box of talcum powder. In those days powder was packaged in a box the size of a chocolate box and the lid could be removed so you could smell the product before you purchased it. Frank noticed Sophie, a big-busted middle-aged lady who wore loose-fitting dresses and open coats to cover her corpulent body. She smelled the powder, put the lid back on, then slid the box down the front of her dress between her breasts.

At the new cash register, she paid for a small number of groceries and was just ready to pick up her purse and walk out the door, when Frank looked her in the eye, then at her breasts, and asked, "Mrs. Fitzgerald, would you like to pay for the talcum powder?"

Frank did not anticipate what would happen next.

With a grunt and a shrug of her shoulders, she grabbed the box from its hiding place, slammed it on the counter, and hustled out the door as quickly as she could move.

Frank looked down after she had left, and on the counter was the lid of the box and from the counter on out of the door was a trail of white powder.

That night at closing, Frank had everyone on the floor in stitches as he retold the story.

Competition was fierce. Not only was there another store in town but there were also grocery stores in every village and bigger stores were opening in cities. Loblaws opened up a huge self-serve store on George Street in Peterborough. The selection seemed mind - boggling. In the sixties, a family could purchase groceries for a week for less than twenty dollars.

Art and Edna Watkins' grocery store on the road to Havelock attracted customers by selling ice cream cones and top quality meat. After a family bought their groceries on Friday night or Saturday, they would buy huge ice cream cones for six cents each and much larger ones for twelve cents. These cones were sold at cost, but they did bring customers in to purchase their weekly staples. Art and Edna were ahead of McDonald's. They knew kids would pull their parents into this store.

Competition and the banks drove many small grocery stores out of business. In Norwood, the Royal Bank of Canada had just transferred in a new young manager. In cities, small stores were going under; self-serve stores were taking the customers away. Small stores carried the cost of their inventories with banks and when these stores closed their doors, banks were left holding an uncollectible debt. Banks, in their wisdom, brought in a new policy which stated that all privately-run grocery stores would no longer be able to borrow money using their inventories as collateral. This new bank rule drove small stores out of the grocery business and competition closed the door on the other small store in town too. Frank's parents' store had no loans or debts and it was the only one left standing.

After work one Friday, Rusty and his dad were cutting and folding cardboard boxes and Rusty turned to his dad. "Dad, we are the only grocery store left in town, what has happened to all the other stores? Stores are closing in Havelock and Hastings as well."

Arnold, "Your mom can explain it the best, it's not about selling groceries it is more about finance."

Just then Barbara was pushing the doors open with a cart load of empty bottles.

Arnold, "Barb, Rusty just asked me about the other small stores going out of business, can you tell him what is going on behind the scenes?"

Barbara, "Sure let's talk over supper I have to get these empties sorted as they have changed the pick up and delivery times again. The truck is on it its way.

Arnold, "Rusty, give your mom a hand and we will talk tonight over dinner."

As it turned out dinner was interrupted and everyone was involved in helping the new truck driver load and unload. Saturday as usual Uncle Carey and Aunt Bethany were arriving to play euchre for the evening. Rusty and Frank were always happy to see their aunt and uncle.

Barbara, "Boys stay a few minutes and Beth and I will give you our view of the situation." Barb explained to Carey and Bethany the question that Rusty asked and the discussion started. Euchre is one of those card games that you can talk and play at the same time. Not like bridge or canasta. The ladies played the men and the score was kept.

"Beth, you start, as the boys hear my voice too much."

Bethany, "Well, the large grocery stores have market power and they can force the suppliers, big and small to give them thirty or sixty days to pay their bills. Net 30 or Net 60 kills the small suppliers as they do not have the cash flow to finance their sales and wait to be paid. The big stores have the goods sold before they have to pay for them. Their cost of inventory is zero; they have a positive cash flow with no interest costs. The small store does not have the clout and they must pay up front or within a week and if they do not have money they have to finance their inventory, which means paying interest. The large stores buy in bulk and can therefore sell for less than the small stores. They carry a larger selection of goods and they are taking the customers from the small stores. The small stores sell less and can't pay the banks. The bank is then left holding the debt that they can't collect. The banks are in business to take deposits, your money and they lend it out. The difference in what they pay you and what they charge, called the spread, is how they make money. The banks made a rule that they would no longer finance small grocery store inventories and overnight, many stores are out of business. They have come to us for financing and we are in the same position as banks. Whoever has the power makes the rules. Boys, the sad thing is the power is in the hands of the shopper and they don't know it. Every time they spend a dollar they are voting for that product and that store where they bought it."

Barbara, "We have to carry bread and pastries in our store and just down the street the bake shop is suffering and will be out of business soon. Customers want sliced bread and the convenience of picking everything up at once. We still buy our own personal bread from the bakery but the consumer is not always interested in quality as they are often blinded by price. We can't carry the bake shop bread for nothing and the margin we need to cover costs is their profit. They would be working for nothing if they sold their products to us for resale. We watch the ads on television and you can see next week when a new product comes on the TV consumers are in the store and they want to buy it. Give the consumers what they want and the world will change, not always for the better."

Bethany, "If you want to talk about real power, the Liquor Control Board is a government monopoly and they have absolute power over their suppliers. My friend Rita was telling me the other day, her husband Steven works for a large Liquor company, and the LCBO has changed the playing rules again. The small wine producers from Europe that sell to the LCBO get paid ninety days after the last bottle is sold." The winery, a farmer, grows the grapes, harvests, makes the wine, ages it, bottles it, ships it and then they wait for the government to sell everything to the last bottle. As if that was not enough, they then wait another ninety days before the government cuts a cheque. That is power in the market place. You can understand why many small producers in Europe refer to the LCBO as the Large Canadian Bullies from Ontario. They can't and will not sell to them. If you want good wine from small producers drive to Quebec."

Bethany, "Boys I have to start paying attention we are getting behind, but just one last comment. It cost about the same to produce a bottle of cheap wine or a bottle of vinegar. Same process, same equipment. The difference in price is the LCBO profit."

Barb put the last heart, a ten spot on the Ace of clubs and whispered, "Euchre, that will cost you a quarter. Arnold can you open up that nice French red wine, the Burgundy we just purchased in Quebec?"

Rusty and Frank just laughed as for years they watched the Saturday night euchre ritual and either their dad or their mom at the end of the evening would fill the one euchre jar back up with quarters.

Rusty would turn to Frank, "That's why mom and her sister are in finance."

Rusty finished his high school education and decided he did not want to follow in his parents' footsteps. Watching and helping his parents toil Monday to Saturday just to have Sunday morning off, and then go back in the afternoon to prepare for Monday's opening was too much. Evenings, his dad spent moving paper in the office. There had to be a better way to make a living, so he could have time to do some of the things he wanted to do. Rusty was no coward to hard work and responsibility. He had a lot to offer.

His mom on Wednesdays joined her sister. They were both chartered accountants and his aunt worked full time for the small finance company in Peterborough. Maybe having two or more part time jobs would be better than one thought Rusty.

Arnold happened to be talking to Manley one day when he came in to pick up some ribs. Arnold also sold complete ribs. These ribs were not cut into back and side pieces, you got the full rib. That was what farmers were used to and wanted.

"Hi Manley, what can I get you today?"

"I need a large bunch of ribs to fill a roasting pan. We have company coming on Saturday."

"Come back Friday night at closing and I will have fresh ribs for you. If you are late, just knock on the door as we will be cleaning up."

"I hear Rusty is not going on to university. I guess he will be in here full-time?"

"Heck no, he is not interested in staying here. He's looking for another job."

"See you Friday."

Within a week the local Member of Parliament for the province dropped in and Arnold could see he wanted to have a chat.

"Come on into the back while I cut up the next quarter, and don't stand too close or you could get that white shirt dirty for a change." Long-time friends could tease each other with neither one getting his back up.

"Arnold, Rusty your oldest is not coming into the business?"

"Yep, wants to strike out on his own for a while. He just might find out what the world is like and come back with a different view of the grocery business. He just needs a change."

"You might want to tell Rusty that the Brewers Retail store in Havelock is looking for a strong young man to replace old Phil. He turned sixty-five and is retiring next month. They need a young man in there, especially on the loading docks, and then he can work his way up. You know they have benefits. Ralph is the new manager."

Benefits were something Arnold could only dream about. In your own business you put away for the future or you worked until you dropped.

"Thanks, Roger. I will mention it to him."

That is how things work in a small town, one hand washes the other and everyone looks out for each other.

Last Thanksgiving, Roger had been standing in exactly the same spot when he mentioned to Arnold that the McGee family were in tough times and there would be no turkey on their table for the holiday. It just so happened that the mail man for that rural route later dropped off a twenty-five pound turkey. When asked, he said, "I have no idea where it came from." Roger and Arnold had split the cost.

Rusty drove over and met with the Brewers' manager. Everything was going fine until Rusty's age came up. You had to be twenty-one to work in a store that sold alcohol. Rusty was hired as long as he stayed at the back out of sight. Rules in those days were viewed only as guidelines and were meant to be bent. Within a few months, Rusty was running the complete store and it was humming.

Operating a beer store was simple. You had only one product and it came in bottles of the same height. Each case held six, twelve, or twenty-four bottles. Rusty's experience in the grocery store proved to be invaluable. The loading platform was soon dug deeper, wheeled dollies were made, and floor-to-ceiling shelving was bolted against the walls. Shelving, roller trays, and everything needed for the return of bottles was made so the employees could handle any size and shape of bottle and case.

Ralph was not sure why Rusty was designing and building stuff that did not exactly fit the cases. When the stubby brown bottle was phased out, Ralph finally understood.

Customers nicknamed every Brewers Retail store the "Beer Store." Another name was the "IN and OUT" store. Those were the two most prominent signs customers saw when going to the store. The lesson of those signs would not be lost on Rusty.

Beer Store employees called their stores the "IN - IN, OUT - OUT stores. In comes the customer, in comes the empties, out go the full empties, and out goes the customer.

Bottle returns were a pain at best. Soggy boxes, half-full, smelly, you name it, they were all taken back and the refund of two cents per bottle was given to the customer.

In no time Rusty had the empties organized too and skid after skid was built to store those. Once a truck delivered fresh beer, the empties were quickly loaded and the truck pulled away. Ralph admired the drive and interest Rusty was showing in the business and took him under his wing. By then, Rusty was helping Ralph with the paperwork, and a short time later, he was doing it all and Ralph just added the signature.

Not only was Rusty fast and accurate with numbers, but he also saw patterns quickly. Rusty, using beer-in and empties-out, could estimate bottle trippage. Bottles were refilled on average eighteen times. The cost of a new bottle plus cleaning was spread over eighteen sales. Bottle trippage for beer bottles was much higher than that of pop bottles from the grocery store. Barbara would remind the boys to look behind the numbers. "Numbers give you information if you can see the flow and the patterns."

Within two months of Rusty taking over the paperwork, he checked the figures and cases over and over again, and he knew there was a shortage. Either cash or empty bottles were going missing. There was a leak somewhere. Growing up in the family grocery store, he had been in charge of pop bottle returns. His mom had taught him well.

Rusty marked and counted empty cases in the back room after all the employees had left for the day. He had a mental checklist that he went down, one item at a time. The cases were not what was disappearing, he concluded. The next step was to balance the cash-return till at the end of each day. Once the float was taken out, the till should match the value of the bottles on the skid within a few dollars. Every day they matched. "Maybe I am wrong", he thought.

Two weeks later on Saturday the back storage room was full of empties. Pallets were overflowing with cases on the floor and into the aisles. Monday, the truck was coming and he either had to sort the empties now or come in early Monday morning.

"Don't be asked twice," rang in his ears.

The cases were sorted, counted, and marked. The cash till for the empties, minus the float was counted and it was short ten dollars and twenty-five cents.

A case of empties was forty-eight cents. That times twenty cases would be nine dollars and sixty cents.

Rusty thought, that can happen once in a while. Let's see if there's a pattern.

He double-checked the work roster for Saturday and made a list of five names. Beside the date and names he wrote ten dollars and twenty five cents short.

Every day Rusty counted cases and balanced the cash paid out for the empties.

A pattern soon emerged. When the storage area was overflowing and cases were stacked everywhere, about ten dollars and change would be short in the till. Saturday was the day.

To catch someone putting ten dollars in their pocket during an eight-hour shift is nearly impossible. How could he narrow down the odds?

Ralph, the store manager, never worked the return line and did not handle the cash from that till. Rusty would take Ralph into his confidence.

The next Monday morning after the fresh beer was packed away both men were at the front counter. This was a slow time.

"Ralph, I got something to tell you."

Ralph immediately went into panic mode and perspiration began to collect underneath his arms. He was afraid that Rusty was going to hand in his resignation. *Maybe I have been working him too hard.*

Ralph's eyes blinked and Rusty continued.

"Ralph, I have been checking the empties and the cash desk that we use for the empties and there is a pattern. The cash is short every Saturday.

"How much?"

Rusty handed Ralph a copy going back sixteen weeks.

"I have never checked the empties with the till and head office is very sloppy on this side of the business. How do you know the till is short?"

Rusty brought Ralph up-to-date and then waited for Ralph to make the next move.

The mixing of shifts had narrowed it down to Dick Hammer."

"Do you have a plan?"

Two customers pushed the door open, walked over, and dropped their empties on the counter.

Twenty-four Labatt 50's later, two happy customers went out the door.

"First, we have to find out how the money is leaving the till and how it is going out the door. Employees are not asked to leave their wallets in the change room so they can just say the ten dollars is theirs. We have to see them in action."

Rusty said, "I am going to change the cash drawer at lunch time and balance with the empties. A new till for the afternoon and a balance at the end of the day will determine if the money is going out in the morning or afternoon. Once we have narrowed it down, I will work that shift helping out. I am the junior guy in the store and it should not throw anyone off".

The next Saturday, the two checks were done and the money went short in the afternoon till. Saturday at closing, everyone would check the next weeks' roster before going home. Dick was down on the schedule Saturday afternoon helping on the return station.

The first Saturday afternoon Rusty saw nothing, but he kept a mental count of everyone he knew and didn't know returning empties. Dick's sister came in at the end of the day with a grocery bag half-filled with bottles. She folded and placed the empty bag in her shoulder purse. She bought a case of twenty-four to take home. Most women purchased only twelve as a case of twenty-four was a good lift.

His mind turned over and over. Most of the customers brought back full cases and the other half would have odd numbers in grocery boxes or bags. Dick would look into the bag or box and say fourteen cents, twenty cents, or whatever number of empties he counted times two cents. He only missed counting correctly twice in the afternoon.

After closing on Saturday, Ralph and Rusty balanced the tills and the empties and, sure enough, the till was ten dollars and thirty-five cents short. In the sixties beer truck drivers would drop the odd case and they would mark it on their invoice as breakage. Ralph, like most store managers, never had to buy his own beer.

This Saturday, Ralph and Rusty were having a beer before going home. As Rusty was bringing Ralph up-to-date, he described the customers he did not know and tried to place names with faces.

The lights went on for Rusty; he thought he knew how the money was disappearing.

Next Saturday afternoon he counted the loose bottles after Dick had handed out the money, and he soon discovered that if there were more than ten loose bottles in a bag or box, Dick was counting one or two less and shorting the customer.

No customer caught him that day. When Dick's sister came in again with her bag of bottles, Rusty saw Dick folding the bag and handing it back. Rusty was sure he saw six two-dollar bills go into the bag. Two dollar bills are brown and almost the same colour as the bag so it was hard to tell.

Dick was not only taking ten dollars, he was shorting the customers on the empties.

The Saturday roster went up and Rusty was on as helper three times the following week.

All three days Rusty counted while carrying the empties back to the storage room. Dick was shorting one or two bottles for most broken cases.

Pennies add up to dollars, and in those days a weekly wage was sixty-five dollars. Rusty estimated that with the ten dollars taken on Saturdays, plus the amount earned on weekly bottle shortages, Dick was doubling his salary.

Not leaving a stone unturned, Rusty decided the next week to assist on the sales counter and check to see what was happening there. Dick was helping out his family once again. They would order and pay for a twelve-pack, while a case of twenty-four was going out the door. The inventory system that was in place was on cases and was not broken down to size. A small slippage would not show up on any of the paper work.

Rusty and Ralph had a talk. Ralph had never fired anybody in his life and was apprehensive about doing this the first time. Ralph knew he had to inform his supervisor and present the evidence if required. He understood completely that the store manager was the person who hired and fired.

Ralph didn't sleep all of Saturday night. He was worried sick and in his mind went through all the different scenarios and none were going to be pleasant. The phone rang at ten-thirty Sunday morning.

"Hi Ralph, it's Rusty."

"Do you have your radio on?"

"No, why?"

"Dick Hammer and his sister were killed last night in a car accident. The radio report said four people heading west turned left at Fowlers Corners on Highway Seven. The eastbound car hit them broadside in the intersection. Three died at the scene and the fourth died at the hospital. It seems they were at the Red Barn dance and were heading home in the rainstorm."

THE POWER OF ADVERTISING

Rusty always remembered the "IN and OUT" signs and how they trained customers to come in one side of the parking lot and leave on the other side. One day he got to prove to everyone that advertising really works.

When head office shipped a full truck of beer that they had not ordered, Rusty had a plan.

One Tuesday morning, at ten-thirty sharp, Ralph said, "Rusty, looks like we are getting another unexpected shipment."

Rusty replied, "Guess they have to move some old inventory."

The back door of the beer store was unlocked and swung open so the tractor trailer could back in under the overhang. The trailer door seal was cut, the trailer backed in, and the doors were opened. The end pallets were filled with Wye Valley Hereford Pale Ale beer. Sales had plummeted after the news had broken in Quebec. (Two Saturday night drinkers had consumed over twenty four bottles of Wye Valley and had died in their sleep. The competing beer companies had jumped on the news and behind the scenes spread it as far and as wide as possible. Sales of Wye Valley plummeted.)

"Oh well, a few skids won't hurt."

Bud, the driver broke the news. "Sorry guys, you are only getting half the trailer," and he smirked.

Ralph and Rusty looked at each other.

All their empties were to be loaded into the now half-empty truck. Ralph wondered why Fargo was pulling out the empty Wye cases.

Rusty remembered how effectively the In and Out signs moved traffic. Rusty also remembered the day his younger brother in his parents' store had pencilled in two extra zeros on the order to Orange Crush in the dead of winter.

Rusty suggested, "I have an idea. Hope you don't mind breaking a few rules."

Ralph, "We'll join the crowd at head office."

Rusty walked back into the storage room and wheeled out empty cases. He piled the empty cases from the floor to the ceiling beside the return desk. New cases of Wye were stacked floor to ceiling beside the sales register.

All the store employees were informed that, when they were asked about the Wye cases, they should tell their friends that bad press was causing some loyal beer drinkers to stock up, as they feared the company might stop making Wye. Limit your friends to only two cases. Head office has only sent us half a trailer of Wye on Tuesday. That was a special order.

Within a week Rusty and Ralph were ordering more Wye. Head office was in shock and had to know why one store in their empire was ordering more!

Big Mack pulled his Ninety-Eight Olds into the parking lot first thing Monday morning.

Ralph looked out with dreaded horror. This was a surprise inspection. Once a year, he thought, was enough.

"Hey Ralph, what is going on in your parking lot? It's so clean I can't find a cap anywhere."

Colin MacKenzie was called big Mack, as he was large, talked loudly, and carried a big stick.

Big Mack soon discovered who was behind the clean lot, the conveyor system for empties, the flex shelving, and the deep truck ramp.

Big Mack told Ralph that his store had the largest percent increase in sales of all the stores in Southern Ontario and also his store labour costs had fallen. Ralph showed Big Mack the back door that was set up for returns every Monday nights after closing.

"Colin, Rusty has all the guys back in their half-ton trucks Monday after work on their way home. They unload their empties from weekend stag parties and cash out in fresh beer. Rusty adjusts the sales and returns figures on Tuesday's books. All the kids collecting bottles return their empties Monday as well. Rusty is a hero to those kids. Sunday morning before church they hit all the outdoor party spots and clean up beer bottles. Rusty also tells them where they can sell empty liquor and wine bottles.

"Ralph, I have to meet this guy Rusty. Is his name Rusty or FARGO? Was he the chap that caught Dick?"

"Rusty comes in late on Mondays and leaves late after the empties are stacked away. Fargo is Rusty's nickname. He drives an old Fargo half-ton truck."

When Rusty was seventeen, he had bought his first vehicle from his Uncle's used car lot. She was old but in good shape. "FARGO" was still starting every morning and running smooth. Carrying bottles, not girlfriends, made that purchase decision. He also found out that the girls liked trucks as well. The key was that you had wheels.

Big Mack arrived back at head office Tuesday and the first thing he did was pull out the promotion sheet. Where and when was the next store manager's position open? He then walked down the hall to his secretary and informed her that he needed Rusty's file.

Big Mack just stared at the birth date. January 15, 1944. This was September 1964. Rusty was a minor! Ralph had hired a minor and he was just about to promote a minor.

He tipped his chair back and started to laugh so hard that tears came to his eyes. He knew he had just met his future boss; he was not sure how long it would take him.

Big Mack had no intentions of moving up the corporate ladder but he sure could pull strings for good people below his level. Big Mack had already moved some of his people up the ladder past him and into the corner offices. This would be fun and would make his job interesting. Big Mack had power up and down in the organization.

Rusty's younger brother, Frank, was going to school full-time and slugging in the hours at the family grocery store. Frank enjoyed talking to their customers, old and young alike.

Mrs. Cutcliff was a character with lots of spunk.

Mrs. Cutcliff was the oldest living lady in Norwood, and was upset that she could not buy a bottle of sherry, something she enjoyed at the end of a day, in her own hometown. When she was in her nineties, the local paper, the *Norwood Register*, made the mistake of interviewing her in public when she was downtown shopping for her groceries. In public, in front of a number of local citizens she was asked the question on her views of the upcoming vote on allowing a liquor or beer store in town.

Very clearly, in a voice that was not loud or meant to be heard by eavesdroppers, she said, "You know I am getting on in age and before I die I want to walk downtown in Norwood, my town, and buy my bottle of sherry and go home and pour myself a glass before supper."

The story was carried in the *Norwood Register* and the next vote ushered in the mandate for Norwood to become wet again after years of being dry. The good news was that Mrs. Cutcliff did walk downtown to buy her sherry before she was too old to enjoy her daily reward for living and working so long. She walked back home after that, and for many evenings, she poured herself one serving before supper.

The next time Mrs. Cutcliff came into the store, Frank had her favourite butter tarts, homemade, in a gift box. Frank knew she had a sweet tooth and she always bought butter tarts at the church fundraising sales. Frank had followed his mom's recipe to a tee.

In Ontario the idea of having beer and wine conveniently available to the public and tourists in grocery stores was not allowed in the 60's and 70's." The underlying belief is that we do not want our children exposed to alcohol.

During the sixties, teenagers had access to bootleggers through older brothers and sisters. Getting booze was the easy part; getting the money was harder.

Today an average teenager is approached daily in high school to purchase a variety of street drugs on the spot. That is why some people call high schools "High" schools. *You can get a high from the dealer whose locker is next to yours with no ID, no age requirement, and no discrimination. If you have the money, you get the drugs. Private schools with high income students are a drug pusher's dream.*

Frank was nineteen when he finished with high school. Even though Frank had the marks to continue on to university, he lacked the compulsory language credit to get in. Universities across Canada required a second language credit and this barrier blocked many students from continuing on to higher learning. When Frank dropped French in grade eleven he knew he would not be able to go to university.

Frank had his first interview with the LCBO manager in Peterborough, but because he was only nineteen, he was told that he had to wait until he reached twenty-one to work there.

Frank was anxious to leave the family business and try something new. He could always fall back on the grocery store business, as large new chain stores were desperate for experienced staff and they paid managers well.

In the meantime, selling used trucks and used cars looked like a sure way to have fun and make money. He was used to evening and weekend work and he wouldn't have to stock shelves and clean, clean, and do more cleaning.

Frank talked to his mom and dad after cleaning up one evening.

Arnold was not surprised that Frank wanted to try something new. Rusty was having fun at the Breweries and he knew he would be losing his other right arm soon.

Rusty At Head Office.

Since the Alcohol and Gaming Commission of Ontario (AGCO) made and enforced the rules, it was allowing foreign ales and beers to be sold in the LCBO stores across the province. Premium and regular offshore beers commanded a higher price and generated larger profit margins. The LCBO decision makers were happy to build more shelf space for these items. They were indifferent to Brewers' Retail and stated that it was not their problem if those stores' sales would be affected. Since Brewers' Retail could not carry or sell any of the products liquor stores were carrying, they knew there would be no retaliation in the marketplace.

Fargo, Rusty, watched as foreign beer sales started to increase. Many beer store customers were trying to hide non-returnable foreign bottles from LCBO stores in their domestic cases for refunds. The Ontario government was not only after higher profits, their thirst for greater profits encouraged more non-returnable bottles.

Rusty talked to his assistants and his boss Randy and decided on a plan.

Rusty and his small staff got the data and calculated all foreign beer sales for the last three years. The numbers were crunched.

Rusty said, "If we can persuade the AGCO to make a rule that all offshore beer companies have to use Ontario bottles or bottles identical to Ontario's, it would solve a number of problems. The first one would be that the beer store would pay for the returns. Secondly, the influx of new bottles would provide free bottles for domestic brewers. One simple change would stop millions of tons of glass going into the dump."

Rusty's big boss, Alfred, the vice president, took him to one side.

Over lunch, Alfred made sure Randy, Rusty and his assistant Big Mack were all together to get the same message.

"Boys, don't get your hopes up too high. Remember Brewers Retail is owned by the big beer companies, so we are not on a level playing field with the government-owned and operated LCBO. The LCBO and AGCO work together. Remember that bottle manufacturers have hired a number of retired AGCO staff and some of our people as well."

Foreign beer companies had deep pockets and they provided a number of annual junkets for LCBO executives. These trips included sightseeing, and all the perks of a luxury holiday for the executives and their spouses. If questioned, they were just doing business.

Foreign beer companies will not want to change their bottles or use a label, as we do. These changes will cut into their markets and profits. AGCO executives are not interested in promoting Canadian business, let alone the breweries.

Alfred added, "Look what they do to the Ontario and Canadian wine industry. The LCBO buyers shop the world and bring in foreign wines and alcohol, providing thousands of jobs for other citizens. Can you imagine, for a minute, French, German, or Italian governments promoting Canadian wine and beers? Their producers and countrymen would have old guillotines and firing squads dusted off pretty quickly.

Try to find a Canadian product when you travel abroad. I guess I am getting off topic."

Big Mack responded, "Alfred, you tell it like it is."

Rusty just sat and soaked in all the information. "The day will come," he thought. "Be patient."

Three weeks later, Rusty was invited on a trip to Japan to tour a large beer company. The AGCO travelling partners were taking their spouses and Rusty was encouraged to do the same.

Rusty wondered if another beer company was up for sale or was this their way to fold him into the club.

Rusty's mind began to wonder about the discussion that must have taken place when public pressure was forcing the LCBO to solve the problem with throw away liquor and wine bottles. The AGCO Alcohol and Gamming Commission of Ontario and the LCBO are government owned and operated. The Brewers Retail business is privately owned but ruled by the AGCO. Who wants to collect bottles and handle the mess that it entails? He was sure the playing field at the bargaining table was level. The LCBO collects the deposit money and the Brewers collects the bottles. That is how government monopolies Partner.

The bonus plan for the LCBO executives would not be harmed by this arrangement: was Rusty's thinking.

Frank Gets A Car.

Since Frank needed a car he asked his brother to take him into town. Frank remembered his brother's buying experience when he got his Fargo. Rusty had taken his younger brother along. Rusty just enjoyed teaching his younger brother, Frank.

Rusty teased, "Frank, you just want a ride in the Fargo."

"No, I would like you to come, as I want to buy a car and ask Uncle Carey if he needs to hire someone."

"Do you want to become a used car salesman?"

"I want a change from the grocery store."

"Have you told mom and dad? You know they wanted both of us to stay in the grocery business and maybe someday take over the Norwood store?"

"I think they knew ahead of me."

Sunday afternoon they went into Peterborough after lunch. Uncle Carey was busy washing a two-year-old truck when the two nephews pulled in and parked the Fargo.

Carey asked, "How are my favourite nephews today?"

Rusty chuckled, "Uncle, you lie like a cheap rug, you tell all of us the same thing."

They all laughed.

Carey Ford owned and operated one of the largest used car and truck lots in Peterborough. The sign out front just said, "Used Cars" and in the bottom corner

Carey Ford and Father.

The boys' father, Arnold, and Carey had been buddies growing up on adjoining farms in Cottesloe. They rode the school bus together and were in the same grade, but not necessarily the same class, until grade ten.

Carey's dad died at the supper table when Carey was sixteen. He reluctantly left school and ran the family beef farm. His older sister Gail and his mom comprised the labour force.

At the age of nineteen his mom remarried into money, and his sister tied the knot a week later.

Carey rented out the farm and sold the livestock and equipment, keeping only the tractor and small equipment for the house garden. He lived in the big farm house by himself.

Carey got a job driving the parts truck for an auto parts company as he wanted to find out how the industry worked and he figured this would be the best way to meet all the players.

He saved every penny he could and, at the age of twenty, he started selling used cars. Selling on commission, you needed to have a bit of savings and then budget your money for those inevitable slow months. At age twenty-five he purchased the used car lot from his boss, who was retiring. Within five years he had built the Norwood lot up to a good size, sold it to his top mechanic, and opened up a larger lot in Peterborough.

Carey leased this large lot beside a new car dealer and financed his small inventory with loans and personal savings.

The car business is dead simple. Buy a vehicle at the correct price, cover your costs, and sell it, making between $100 and $200 per car.

Inventory was sourced from five main streams. New car dealers did not want high mileage vehicles and they would wholesale them off their lots to used car dealers. Executors cleaning up estates often had vehicles to cash out. Undertakers were valuable contacts. Oshawa and Toronto had large wholesale auction houses. Past customers trading up were the best source for buying and selling vehicles. A new and growing source was the leasing market. Business cars were being leased so companies did not have to tie up their capital. At the end of the lease customers wanted to move onto a new vehicle and more and more leased cars were on the market.

Carey liked being beside a huge, successful new car dealership. They got to sell the car once, when it was new. He could sell the same car three or four times, and when he added up the servicing and the parts costs, it would often total more than a new car. Carey liked not having to report to head office and to the owners of a dealership. He was his own boss.

Carey had a number of things going for him. He hired the best mechanics and paid them the going rates that they would be paid at a dealership. The mechanics also got a car off the lot to drive. What better way to have a used car diagnosed and fixed. The sales staff and office staff all drove a used car from the lot.

Most of the sales staff were part time and wanted to work evenings and weekends. Carey went against the grain and hired mostly teachers and young undertakers. He had discovered that these two groups of people knew everybody in the community and were trusted. They were honest, had manners, and treated everyone with respect. Teachers and retired teachers had connections with students heading out to university or their first jobs. Many students needed wheels and had very little money.

The staff was trained by Carey. He trained the mechanics to sell, the office staff to sell, and his sales staff to sell. When a car or truck was sold, every staff member received five dollars extra on their Friday pay. If it was a repeat customer, the bonus was ten dollars. Carey believed that everyone on the lot had been involved in the selling of a car.

Carey constantly reminded his staff, "We do not sell cars and trucks. We fill the needs of our customers. If we can not help them, it is our job to point them in the correct direction."

A file folder was kept on every customer who purchased a car or truck. On the left side was all the customer information and on the right all the car information. Every time the customer came in for servicing or parts the visit was recorded. Telephone numbers, addresses, and changes in families were all recorded.

Carey and Arnold were best men for each other's weddings. They married identical twin sisters, Barbara and Bethany Brooks. The two B's were the youngest of eight children.

Arnold had suggested that Frank talk to his uncle. "You might like selling cars."

When a customer came in, the sales staff was instructed to find out as much as they could about the customers' needs and wants and put them into two separate categories. If you could not meet their needs, tell them up front and guide them to where they should go. If you could meet their needs and hit most of the wants, you had a chance of making a sale.

Numerous customers were advised that they should be purchasing a new car, and a phone call to the sales manager at the new car lot next door ensured that they would get a warm welcome. They left with the promise that, when they were dealing again, "Please come back, as we would like to give you a price on the car you are selling and we can also service your new car. We want happy customers that will keep returning and also will service their cars here." Like the hotel chain whose motto was "The best surprise is no surprise", Carey's staff was instilling trust and honesty into their relationships with customers. Friends who did not buy their car at Carey's envied the special treatment Carey's customers got, and next time would think about buying there.

Every car that was sold had an extensive checklist covering all the moving parts, worn parts, and body conditions. The customer knew up front that in twenty thousand miles, new tires would be needed, or that in sixteen months, a new muffler would likely have to be put on.

After the sale of a car, the customer was not forgotten. The wash bay was open Saturday and Sunday, and customers could use it free of charge. The two bays were kept busy year round. The bay with the pit, legal in those days, was available if you wanted to service your own car. Oil changes, grease jobs, and other minor repairs were encouraged. The parts counter was kept busy with mechanics and customers ordering parts and supplies for their cars. The mechanics would often stop by and give customers advice if asked.

"Uncle Carey I am looking for a car and a job," said Frank.

"You have come to the right place. I need a new employee and every staff member drives one of our cars. Let's talk."

Frank's education would be starting on Monday morning at seven-thirty. He drove home the oldest car on the lot, a Studebaker, which someone had just turned in on a newer Ford.

Monday Morning

Frank pulled the Studebaker into the employee lot at seven-fifteen and found his uncle filling the two pop machines in front of the office. These coin-operated machines were placed outside from spring to freeze-up. They were wheeled inside during the winter months and were plugged in beside the wash bay area. The cash from the Coca-Cola and Canada Dry machines was enough to pay for three one-week trips during the year. Carey and Gail would go to a different country each trip to visit a car-manufacturing plant. The plant visits were all prearranged and the two of them were treated well, and also with some curiosity, as no new dealers and certainly not used car dealers paid their own way to come and tour facilities. The trips were all tax-deductible expenses and photographs taken were proudly displayed on the walls of the sales office. Credibility was established once a customer saw the gallery of manufacturers' pictures.

Carey greeted him, "Hi Frank. Come with me after you put your lunch in the refrigerator. We will walk the lot."

On the way to the refrigerator, Frank noticed the coffee was already made and the office had been cleaned from top to bottom and it smelled fresh. Two auto body mechanics were helping themselves to coffee and homemade cookies. Frank introduced himself to Ole and Morris. They both worked at the Peterborough Collision and Body shop. They were picking up a truck on their way into work.

Carey had good advice. "Frank, to sell, you must know your product inside and out. Make, model, options, and condition. Every vehicle has a weak spot and some have more than one. I sometimes wish that car company executives would drive their companies' used vehicles, so they would experience first-hand glaring problems."

As they walked the lot, Carey would say where the car came from and what was done on it before the final cleaning. Cars and trucks were organized according to make and descending price. Certain makes and models would be wholesaled out if they had too many hidden problems to correct. Carey did not want his customers to be stuck with lemons. Inevitably, these would come back to haunt him. Nineteen-fifty GMC products would have their fenders rust off, Volkswagen bugs would fall into two pieces with rust, and certain Ford and Chrysler products were prone to electrical problems and were hard to start in rain or cold weather.

"Frank, we have the luxury of not selling junk, while the new car lots have no choice. They must sell all models, and they know or hope the warranty period is long enough and stretches until the customer buys his next new car. When the customer comes back to the dealer for a new car, the dealer knows he is getting trouble as a trade-in so he can't offer much."

"You know, Frank, the car company with the highest price for their used cars will always be the top company. My friend Hector, who works in Oshawa, has told me that the company is starting to shift incompetent managers into Parts and Service. Spend all that money trying to sell the new car, and then screw your customers when they have bought your product. We will always do well in the used car market."

A large board, the shape of the used car lot, hung on the office wall. A pocket on the board showed where each car or truck was parked. The key and tag for each vehicle was in the pocket with the second set in the safe under lockdown.

"Every year we collect all the new car brochures from the dealers. They are in the filing cabinet. When a car comes in, we drop the brochure into the file until it is sold."

As Frank was listening, he made the connection and now understood why his mom was always loaded with pop to go to work on Wednesdays in Peterborough. The Coke truck driver often said to Frank, "You guys are one of my biggest drops."

"Frank, your first job is to check the cars when they come back from the body shop. If the paint is sloppy or not done to your liking, you send it back."

"Once the car comes out of shop, you will test drive it to pick up new plates. If the brakes, steering, shocks, muffler, or any noise or vibration is felt, send it back to our shop."

"Uncle Carey, I guess I am the quality control guy?"

"Every new employee is given this job first. You will get comfortable sending back cars. Remember, every employee before you has had this job."

"Every vehicle gets a new set of premium grade tires. The used tires are sold to our customers when they need a spare or temporary tire."

"When you realize that we are selling quality cars honestly to our customers, the truth will show when you are talking."

"How many times have you overheard stories in the grocery store? Reputations are built one car at a time. If you have one employee saying negative things, you will lose sales. Everyone on the lot sells the car."

Carey pointed out, "For the first week I want you to interview everyone. They are expecting you to ask a lot of questions."

"After I check with the customer, you will tag along and watch me for a week. You will be signing the bottom of the form and earning the sales commission. Take the form home tonight and memorize the front and the back."

Pat, the office secretary, put a sign in the window and Carey knew the phone call was for him.

Frank took out his pad and went down each row of cars and trucks and made a one-page seating plan for vehicles just like he had observed his teachers doing for students.

Frank talked to the two mechanics first.

Wilfred and Delmar introduced themselves when Frank walked in.

"Hi Frank, my name is Willie and this is Del."

They shook hands.

"You are the new guy on the lot?"

"Yes, I am here to learn."

"You have come to the right place. We know all about you and your brother Fargo. We sometimes think Carey is your proud father."

Frank had no idea. His aunt and uncle had no children, so nieces and nephews just filled in the holes.

"When would be a good time to ask you questions?"

"We can walk and talk in here. Take the Studebaker and follow Del. He's driving the Impala over to the body shop. Del can talk on the way back."

Frank realized very quickly that the interview process was working two ways. He was also being evaluated. When Willie and Del and Pat referred customers, they matched them to the sales person that would work with them. Everyone on the lot received a weekly bonus when cars were sold. They wanted to make sure the sales person did not drop the ball.

Carey had exhausted Frank's questions for the day and walked back into the sales office.

"Frank, this is Bob White. Frank is learning the business and he will be tagging along."

"Hi Frank. I know your mom and dad. My wife and I curled with them in the same league until we moved to Omemee."

Frank watched and listened.

Bob had bought the car he was driving from Carey and wanted to trade up.

Willie slipped in, got the keys, and put Bob's car on the hoist.

Carey and Bob talked about curling, their families, and being Canadian, the weather.

When all the socializing was nearing an end, Bob said, "My little company is doing well."

Scraper Blades Inc. manufactured and sold the bottom edge of snow-plough blades and the shoes that were attached to ploughs to keep them from digging into asphalt or gravel roads. The two products were always wearing out and he was always there to sell new ones.

"Carey, I am also considering ordering a new car instead of buying used. I am looking at a new Ford."

"Bob, just give me a minute and I will get the figures for you." Carey went to the file and pulled out a new brochure.

Once Bob saw the numbers of the new car, plus delivery, plus admin fee, plus each option compared to the two-year-old used car, he had his answer. The difference in price would be the down payment on the new hydraulic press he needed in his factory.

Carey didn't need an answer, "Bob, do you mind if I have Frank write up his first sale?"

"Heck no. Frank, if you ever consider selling plough parts, let me know."

Frank watched Carey and the other salesmen sell nine cars that week. Five were repeat customers, three were referrals and one was a walk-in. Three other potential buyers were referred to the Norwood lot, to Cobourg, and one next door to buy a new Chevrolet.

The bonus that week was huge.

Frank commented to Uncle Carey on pay day, "This is a great pay cheque. It sure beats the grocery store."

Carey replied, "In car sales you have some good weeks and many bad weeks. Budget your money and you will never have that hungry look in front of a customer."

Soon Frank was on his own with his desk in the corner of the show room. He had a calculator, pad of paper, and a telephone. His newly-printed business cards were stacked and ready to go.

Local calls were made through the Peterborough phone exchange. Everything outside was long distance. If he went over forty dollars a month, he paid.

Frank shared the walk-in business with the other sales staff, and he averaged one referral a week. Frank learned to use his home phone and business phone to contact friends and relatives to let them know he was selling cars.

Frank was also given the Dead File, made up of customers who had not purchased anything in four years or who had not been in for service for two years. He did not want to use up his entire phone budget, so he decided to mail out a card with a free car wash coupon inside. Frank paid Willie's son fifty cents a wash and customers started to book for Saturday and Sunday washes.

Carey was delighted. "Frank, those coupons are working. A great idea!"

After a time, Frank was picking up two sales a week from the Dead File, plus he was getting many good leads to follow up on. Past customers drifted away when they could find a good mechanic closer to their homes or when a special deal was being promoted by a competitor. A ten-mile radius was usually the limit for a customer to stay loyal and return for most of their service work.

Service by appointment and drop-in service had to work together as these customers had two different sets of needs.

Frank soon hit the numbers and became the top sales person. He noticed that his uncle never signed the contracts. He would always bring in a sales staff to sign and receive the commission. Frank asked his uncle why he never took a sale.

"Frank, I need someone to follow up with the customer and make sure they are happy and will want to return to buy another car. Besides, part-time teachers and morticians need these commissions and they have an excellent retention record with their customers."

The Successful Cheese Maker

Frank learned many lessons watching his uncle and the other sales staff.

The one particular lesson he would use time and time again and it was so typical of a small town:

One day Carey remarked, "We need to take a car back to Sterling. We just got this high-mileage Chevrolet in from the boys in Sterling and they want it back.

Curly, the general manager filled Frank in. Ross, the owner was a cheddar cheese maker and he had saved for a long time to buy a new car. This year he had won a number of awards and along with some prize money was finally able to buy a new Olds. He was Grand Champion at the Royal Winter Fair and the Grand Champion at the London, England's top cheddar show.

However, shortly after he drove his new car to the factory, his retail business suddenly died. Patrons, farmers who owned the co-op and his regular customers saw his new car and figured that he was becoming rich, making too much money. Once Ross realized that his new car was the downfall of his business, he went back to the new car dealer in Sterling and asked for his old car back. He asked Curly to spread the rumour that he could not make the payments.

"Ross, you paid cash."

"Just tell everyone that I can not swing the payments."

Ross got his old car back and the dealer kept the new car on hold.

Margaret, Ross's wife, overheard two ladies gossiping in the grocery store. They were talking about Ross's new car and how much money he was making. When Margaret turned the corner, the two turned their eyes downwards. Needless to say, Margaret followed the line of gossip back to Evelyn, who worked at the bank, and her husband Bruce Richards, the town clerk and treasurer.

After talking to his wife, Ross decided to pay the bank manager a visit. On Monday afternoon at two-thirty, he dropped into the bank.

"Hi Ross."

"Hello, I would like to see Hughie."

"I will tell him you are here."

Ross walked into the manager's office and placed a fresh bag of curd on the manager's desk. Ross and Hughie were both members of the Masonic Lodge.

Ross related the story of Evelyn in the grocery store and her husband Bruce spreading the rumours.

Hughie said, "Ross, leave it with me. This is grounds for dismissal in the bank."

"I think a good scare would be enough. Jobs are hard to get."

"I think two apologies are in order. I, for one, wish to apologize for one of my employees and Evelyn will do the same."

"An apology from Bruce would be better."

Next Saturday afternoon at three, Ross looked up and saw Bruce's car pull into the lot. The side door of the factory opened up and there stood Bruce with a brown paper bag, a liquor bag.

"Ross, I am sorry for making comments about your new car and how much money you are making."

Ross pulled a bottle of Canadian Club out of the bag. It was hard to believe that tight old Bruce had bought a large one.

Bruce asked, "Can I make amends?"

Ross thought for a moment and then he said, "I need a hand today as the girls are busy in the store since business has picked up. If you could give a hand today, I might be able to get out of here by four. My day starts at five in the morning, so it's nice to get home. You can start by helping me cut the cheese for the curd mill."

That day they had two vats of cheese. The first vat had set up and the cheese was ready to be cut. Fresh cheese is about twelve inches thick and needs to be cut into eight-inch strips from one side of the vat to the other. You take a large knife, a bit larger than a machete and twice as heavy. The tip is dull so it does not cut into the vat bottom but the edge is razor-sharp. You use both hands and arms and pull the knife towards yourself through the cheese. The tip of the knife touches the bottom of the vat and the thirty-foot long vat of cheese is cut into the eight-inch strips.

A curd mill fits over the vat. Strips of cheese are picked up and fed down into the curd mill. The curd mill slides down the vat as the cheese strips are fed into the mill. Four long handles are placed on the automatic auger overhead and, just before the machine is started, weighed and measured buckets of salt are spread on top of the curd. Augers mix the curd and salt, automatically trip at the end, and work their way back and forth inside the vat.

"Bruce, you can start cutting the second vat, but first, give me a hand to move the curd mill over to the vat."

The auger is started and, as the salt is mixed in, the whey starts to flow out of the lower end of the vat into the catch drain. The whey from the vat and from the press when the curd is compressed into rounds is pumped back into a stainless steel tank and run through a centrifuge to take out any butter fat. This butter fat is shipped to the butter factory and whey butter is made. Sterling has one of the finest butter factories in Ontario. Whey butter looks like fresh creamery butter but the only difference is that it has a whey or cheddar cheese curd flavor. It is a bit of an acquired taste but once you have had it you will agree with the saying, "Whey butter is way better."

Bruce took his jacket and tie off before cutting the first vat, and by the time the second vat was cut, he was sweating from head to toe.

"Bruce, while the vats are mixing, let's go into the cold room and you can help me open up that bottle of rye."

Bruce, the accountant, thought, "Great. I will get some of that whiskey back."

Ross had his back to Bruce as he mixed cold ginger ale and rye in the wax paper cups.

Bruce would drink fifty percent whisky and fifty percent ginger ale. In the cold storage room with his body sweating, he drank quickly.

The cold storage room was filled with ninety-pound rounds of cheese. Shelves two inches by eighteen inches were built floor-to-ceiling and ran the length of the storage room.

Once a week the rounds were turned over to prevent them from going out of shape as the cheese cured. Turning a ninety-pound cheese was simple, after you got the knack, and have turned a few thousand.

Ross showed Bruce how to do it and he put him to work turning the two lower shelves as he did the harder two upper shelves. All the cheese did not have to be turned that day, but Ross thought the workout would be good for Bruce. He would see how easy it was to make cheese. Three or four drinks later - they went down like water — the men headed back out to the vats to put the curd into the hoops for pressing. By then, Bruce had consumed more than half the bottle. The alcohol wouldn't hit until he went back out into the heat.

Margaret was out there and she had started putting cloth into the hoops. Bruce was handed a bucket and they took turns filling the hoops. Ross laid the full hoop down into the press bed. Today they would use both presses. Once the hydraulics started, more whey came out. Ross made sure Bruce was out of the way before the liquid started to squirt out.

Ross looked at Bruce. "I had better give you a ride home."

Bruce's car remained in the cheese factory parking lot for two days for everyone in the community to see. Bruce, being an accountant, was used to sitting behind a desk and working the cheese pulled just about every stomach and rib muscle known to man. Going from the heat into the cold, getting chilled, then going back into the heat, he not only suffered from a hangover, but he also got a cold. Bruce was in pain every time he coughed.

Evelyn and her friend came Sunday after closing to retrieve Bruce's car.

Bruce never did get the required votes to join the lodge. Some things in small towns never change. They look after each other and there is an unwritten code.

Evelyn kept her job at the bank and her mouth was sealed for the rest of her career.

Two years slipped by very quickly. At age twenty-one Frank could now apply to the LCBO or he could stay selling cars.

Both Carey and his dad encouraged him to follow his dreams.

Frank liked wines and the lure of working for a big organization with set hours and benefits sounded appealing.

Rusty was working his way up the corporate ladder in the beer business and he felt he could do the same in the wine and spirit industry.

Frank dropped into his mother's office on Wednesday to pick her up as her car was staying in overnight to be serviced. Parts would be in on Thursday.

This is when Frank met Katrin.

Katrin was a university accounting student taking a semester off, working part time for his mom and Aunt.

When he set eyes on Katrin, he fell in love. Guys are like that.

Frank did not have any problem chatting up customers, dealers, sales reps, older or younger, but this was different. He finally cleared his throat and said, "Hello."

Katrin looked up, "Hello, you must be Frank?"

"Yes."

"You are here to pick up your mother?"

"Yes."

"Do you say yes to everything?"

"Yes."

They both laughed.

Frank wanted to continue the conversation and stumbled on a plan.

"Friday, a group of us get together after work to play pickup ball. Would you like to come?"

Katrin reached for her arm crutches and pulled them out from under her desk.

"I hope you don't mind if I change a few rules?"

They both laughed.

Katrin lost the use of her legs in a car accident. She was in the front passenger seat when her dad T-boned John Hammer at Fowler's Corners. Doctors thought she would regain most of her leg movements, but it would take time. Each month she was getting more mobility and it looked promising. The more exercise the better.

Frank and his mom talked about Katrin on the way home to Norwood. Nothing was mentioned about Katrin's disability until they were nearing the town limits.

"Frank, you know Katrin can walk only with crutches?"

"Mom, you are looking for life. Katrin glows. She is so positive, she glows. From all the things you have said, she is one of those people who has had a brush with death and every new day is a good day."

Friday came and Frank went to the office to pick up Katrin. She had her ball cap on and a glove in her lap. She was a south paw, left-handed.

"Hi Frank. Where are we playing?"

"Tonight, we are going to Warsaw behind the Senior Public School. The diamond is not being used."

"Hope you don't mind if I play first?" When I play, I have a stick and use it to tag the bag. Do you think that will be okay?"

This was a pick-up game and the score was not important.

Frank switched the low-slung Studebaker for a half-ton truck, which would be easier for Katrin to get into and out of. When Katrin saw the truck, she asked, "Where is the Studebaker? I was looking forward to a ride in that rocket."

Frank was learning not to second-guess and not to compensate.

After the game, they went to friends for a BBQ and beer, and Katrin was quite surprised that Frank had most of his friends drinking wine.

Frank started dating Katrin and fell head over heels.

When Frank asked Katrin for advice on hiring on with LCBO, she would only say, "I am doing what I want to do as best I can. What you do is up to you."

Frank made a decision. "I want to try it and I will give myself five years. When I turn twenty-six, I will decide to stay in or leave."

Frank would make another decision at thirty-one.

Frank applied to the LCBO when he turned twenty-one and was accepted.

On Monday morning, Frank told Carey that he was leaving. "How much notice would you like to have?"

"None, Frank, you are a quick learner and you can come back anytime.

"I would like to come back on my days off and help out."

Chapter Six

Horses On Thin Ice

When he hit the ice with a team of horses, every driver hoped for two things: sharp new shoes on the horses and no weak spots in the ice. When a team of horses or a load fell through the ice, the driver had a serious problem. He was working with very large frightened animals on a slippery surface with little traction. Dropping a sleigh runner through the ice usually meant unloading everything and prying out the sleigh runner with a strong green pole, before driving away. Many times a driver would circle back the next day to get the remaining half-load of logs, wood, or in this story, ice blocks, off the ice. If the whole sleigh went in, the driver had to unhitch the horses quickly before they were pulled backwards into the hole. If this was not possible, their harnesses were cut and the driver hoped for the best.

It was a Friday and everything was running smoothly. The new gas-powered ice machine was cutting the lines long and straight. Men were cross-cutting the long strips into blocks, which they slid along the ice to waiting sleighs. Two men lifted each block onto a sleigh bed. Stakes were jammed in along the bed, so that two layers of blocks could be piled onto the sleigh. That was then driven off the ice and up the road to the ice house.

Handling the horses was a job for the older men, who had reached an age at which they could no longer slug blocks, but they still wanted to contribute. Driving teams takes skill and experience and their supervision of the younger generation on working weekends was needed. Young children did not have the strength to lift the heavy blocks.

Reg's Uncle Bob was a retired farmer who enjoyed being out on the ice to work alongside the men. Bob also liked the farm lunches and suppers that came with being part of a work crew. Living alone was not much fun, especially at meal time.

One afternoon, Bob was getting set to take the second-last load of ice to the ice house. The sleigh was loaded, although not overloaded, and it was nowhere near open water. He was heading down the same ice road that he had travelled on all day. Ice will hold tons, but given too much traffic, it does crack and becomes temporarily unstable. When a load moves across the ice surface, it actually creates a wave in front of the moving sleigh, wagon, or truck. When the ice is thin, one should never travel fast enough to catch that wave. In this case the slow-moving, horse-drawn sleigh was not going fast enough to reach the wave.

About ten yards from land, the ice suddenly gave way and the team and sleigh dropped into the water. Bob yelled and everyone turned in disbelief to see what was happening. Bob jumped onto the back of the horse, Bill, beside the mare, Nellie. These two large black Percherons were brother and sister, not strangers to each other.

Instantly, Bob started to free the horses from the sleigh. He had been in this situation before and he knew exactly what he had to do and do as quickly as possible. In this spot, the pond was too deep for the horses to bottom out and they were in full panic. In some situations, when horses can touch bottom, that becomes even more of a problem, as they will continue to try to jump out, breaking ice and cutting their legs until they are brought under control. Horses are good swimmers, but not in a full set of harness, and certainly not attached to a floating sleigh with ice blocks bobbing around.

Horses talk to each other. Bill and Nellie were letting it be known that they were in trouble. Hearing them, the other team of horses immediately became tense, high-strung, and a challenge to handle.

Reg's uncle knew how to calm the other team, as he had often brought them out of the woods when they caught the scent of a bear. Now, they were as jittery as if they were being ridden by that bear. Talking to them and keeping them moving, even if it was in circles, was needed to get their minds off Bill and Nellie. Horses see out of only one side of their head at a time, so they were driven around in a figure eight, so both sides of their brains could register the situation. Keeping them moving was important. Properly handled, they could do the job of pulling the two horses out of the water.

Everyone on the ice that day was watching Reg for a hand signal or a shout to help get the freezing horses out of the water as quickly as possible. There was no need to consult anyone. Reg was in charge and would tell everyone what to do. He would do it no matter what.

Dropping the sleigh tongue and getting on a set of team whiffletrees was done quickly, and the other team of horses was positioned to pull the mare out first. Ropes were slipped under Nellie and tied to the whiffletree. Just before the horses were given the command to pull her out, Bob put a leather strap around the mare's neck and, with stick in the strap, started to choke her. Nellie's eyes bulged out. She started to suck air in fear of suffocating. Once she started sucking air, in what seemed like minutes but was only seconds, Bob waved and yelled, "Pull." She bobbed out like a cork with no injuries and two men ran her back to the barn. The same choking technique was used on Bill, and soon he was out too and being run back to the barn.

The horses were placed into a box stall together with the team that had pulled them out. They were packed in tightly and blankets were thrown over all four horses. Warm mash was prepared and fed to Bill and Nellie. The other two got a taste only as a reward.

Horses are herd animals and have a well-defined pecking order. Reg had carefully placed the horses together tail-to-nose in the stall so that each groomer horse was beside his or her field partner. Farmers watch their horses to see how they pair off in an open field. Many times two horses will stand close, side by side, with their heads pointing in opposite directions. They are busy rubbing each other and grooming their chosen field companion.

The two horses that had pulled Bill and Nellie out were kept in the same box stall to provide the extra body heat to keep all four warm. Keeping the horses warm and also putting them in their natural social environment was crucial to saving their lives. The two drenched horses needed heat and they also needed comfort to reduce their fears.

Uncle Bob was wet and cold too. He was wrapped in a Buffalo robe and hurried home for a dry change of clothing. Two good shots of rum got his blood warmed and flowing. He sat in the kitchen beside the warm cook stove with his feet on the open oven door. He kept busy talking to the women working around him preparing supper. Friday night was stew night with all the leftovers of the week in one large pot. Fresh homemade bread and freshly-churned butter was used to clean the supper plates and to get everyone ready for homemade pies. Apple pie with cheddar cheese and cherry pie was sitting on the stovetop, off to one side, keeping warm. Tonight there would be homemade ice cream on the pie.

Gloria teased Bob for having taken his Saturday night bath early. She knew the risk that he had taken and the skill that he had needed to get the two horses out of the water. The older generation from the farms had much to offer and in a crisis they had experience that was invaluable. Each person was important in a farm family.

Both horses survived, but Uncle Bob was never forgiven by Nellie. She remembered who had tried to choke her, and whenever Bob went near her, she would bare her teeth and go after him. Bill did not remember so well.

At meal time, everyone had a story to tell about dropping through the ice, but no one had ever heard of choking a horse.

Bob told them about the time he and his dad had to get two horses out of Rotten Lake, when the horses had gone in with a sleigh load of cord wood. The two men had been working alone and did not have another team of horses to help rescue their team. For leverage, his dad quickly cut two curling hacks into the ice, one for each of their boots. After getting the harness around one horse, his dad choked it and the two of them pulled. The first horse out was tied to a stump, so it would not run away. Once both horses were out, Bob rode them back to the barn as quickly as possible. Meanwhile, his dad walked to the nearest farm and got a ride home later that day. They lost one of those two horses that night. Ice-cold water plus fear is a killer. Horses have to want to live and they have to be kept warm and well-fed.

"You know, that's how I got the name Bob. When dad saw me floating in the cold ice water with my red hat on, he said I looked like a fishing bobber and the name stuck. My real name is John." Bob never liked to be called Gramps or Uncle. He preferred the name Bob.

Jack, "Mr. Bob why do you choke horses to get them out of the water?"

Mr. Bob laughed, he forgot that young ears are not experienced ears. "When a horse thinks it is being suffocated it sucks up all the air it can and fills their huge set of lungs. They float higher in the water and they are easier to pull out. I remembered when I split a team in the barn after pulling in a wagon of hay. I was backing them along the full load of hay so we could hitch them to pull the fork. They were harnessed together but in single file. The mare was backing and the horse was heading out and the shaft from the hay drifted down. I was standing in the wrong place and Bill sucked up air and wedged me against the mow wall."

Reg glanced at Gloria, with that hook-line-and-sinker smile.

Mr. Bob explained that warming up their drinking water and giving horses warm mash are both important, but many times it's the boss, their owner, who is the deciding factor. Staying with a horse in the barn overnight has saved many of these magnificent creature's lives. Keeping the lantern on and talking to them and touching them gives them the comfort they need to pull through until daylight. If they survive the night, horses will usually live to work another day.

Young Jack called everyone who was as big as his dad, Mr. or Sir. He called Bob, Mr. Bob. "Mr. Bob, can you tell us a story before you go home?"

"It will have to be a short one 'cause I have to get home and listen to Foster."

Foster Hewitt was the radio station's play-by-play hockey announcer for that night's game and Toronto was hosting the Habs. Bob was a fan of the Montreal Habs. The local Peterborough Petes were a farm team for the Habs.

Mr. Bob continues: "You know we used to milk fifteen shorthorns every morning and every night on the farm. We had a neighbour, Ed Hall, who came from a farm family up the road. They were all cheap. They had the first cent they ever made hidden away in a buried tin can somewhere. Ed worked at the saw mill close to town and each weekday and Saturday afternoon he would drop in to tell some gossip on his way home. I smoked a pipe and always had my leather tobacco pouch in the window of the barn so I wouldn't forget it when we went back to the house for supper."

"At first, when he came in, he would ask if he could have a pipe of tobacco as he had just run out. You know, tobacco was not free, and like a fool I said, 'Help yourself.' Not only would he fill his pipe, but he would pack the tobacco in tightly, so he walked away with as much tobacco as he could. That pipe load would last him until he came back the next day."

"I looked at Mary one day as I saw Bob through the window on his way to the barn, and under my breath, I said, 'Shit, there is Ed.'"

"When he left with another pipeful of my tobacco, I decided this had to stop."

"Then it dawned on me. Dried horse manure looks a lot like tobacco. I scooped up a small shovelful, broke down the buns, and put it on a board in the window of the horse barn. It dried out real quick in the sun and I was soon adding it to the tobacco pouch and mixing it in real well. I started adding manure about November, and by spring, I had Ed on pure horse shit."

"One day, when he was loading his pipe, he made a comment that his pipe was starting to taste a bit sourer."

"Until he died, a few years back, he was known as Shit Head Ed."

"I don't think I killed him."

Little Jack Wilson was in awe. Mr. Bob was his hero.

Epilogue

The next day, the area where the team had broken through was wide-open. A pear-shaped circle, thirty feet at the widest, was just water.

The water main, that was buried under Dummer Road and running north, had cracked and broken wide-open during the night. The running water under the ice was enough to weaken and then melt the surface of the Mill Pond.

Chapter Seven

Walking Backwards You Stand Up Straighter

Life in a small Ontario village in the early fifties was an exciting and turbulent time.

Norwood was getting town water, which meant streets were dug up, town water lines were laid down, and water was piped directly into homes. No more dug or drilled wells, no more basement or crawl space cisterns that collected rain water from eaves troughs, no more hand pumps to get drinking water into a home. With running water in the house, every family had to decide which room would be cut up for a bathroom. A new indoor toilet, sink, and tub meant that the outdoor two-seater would no longer be needed. The weekly ritual of heating water on the wood cookstove and filling a galvanized wash tub for the Saturday bath was coming to an end. The honey pot under the bed would be placed on a dusty shelf in the woodshed, a place that collected many other no-longer-needed gems.

When hot water was limited, and before bathrooms existed, everyone in a family bathed in a wash tub in the kitchen near the woodstove that heated the water. The youngest child bathed first, then the next, and finally up the order to mom, and last came dad. After each bath, a bucket of soapy water would be taken out of the tub and a hot pail put in. Each person would stand up in the tub at the end of the bath and a dipper of fresh, warm water washed off the soap. You would then step out and be towelled down. There were certain advantages to being the youngest. Showers were to be invented later.

Many small villages and towns would put in town water. Flushing toilets, showers and increased consumption of water would overfill the homemade septic tanks and buried drums in the back yard. Communities that were built on top of a flat limestone bed like Lakefield and Bobcageon or a clay non porous soil that is common in the Niagara region soon were floating in waste. Most hand dug wells were soon put out of commission and the call to be hooked up to town water was a necessity. Sewage systems would dig up the roads again.

Propane-fired hot water tanks replaced both the wood-stove reservoirs and the pails of water heating on top of the woodstove. Hot water was there on demand. Electric stoves replaced wood cookstoves. Many a cook said that food would never taste as good prepared on those electric stoves. Wood box stoves were replaced with oil space heaters and wealthier folk installed oil furnaces. Refrigerators were owned by some people. Wall-to-wall carpeting covered cold wood floors and linoleum. Ice houses would soon be replaced and forgotten in this transition period.

This story takes place when ice was still cut in the winter and packed away for summer use. This was in the early

50's in Norwood. Many large farm families had their own ice houses, but people living in villages and other urban centers relied on buying ice in the spring, summer, and fall for their kitchen ice boxes. Each of these wooden ice boxes had a metal tray in the top where a block of ice sat and slowly melted away, keeping everything below it cool. The metal tray had a drain hole that led down to a pan below the ice box. This drip pan had to be emptied before it overflowed onto the floor. Someone in each family was assigned this chore and it was his or her responsibility to empty the pan.

Reg Wilson had been cutting, storing, and selling block ice all his life. This did not represent his family's main income but was a good chunk of it. Reg and Gloria had three daughters and a son who all helped when it was time to cut ice. In the summer time, the children worked on the ice truck delivering blocks to customers in Norwood, Havelock, and Hastings.

The Wilson's largest ice house was forty-feet square. A second older ice house was twenty-feet by thirty-feet. Ice houses were rough buildings with four walls and a roof to keep the sun out and the sawdust in. A foot of sawdust along the outside wall of the building and layers of sawdust between the ice blocks kept them frozen all summer long. Ice houses were usually built on a slight knoll, and they had a layer of coarse gravel underneath to allow for good drainage. If the ice blocks did start to melt a little, the melt water would drain away, rather than pool and increase the rate of melting.

To have enough ice on hand for their two hundred and fifty customers, Reg's family would need to cut and store at least twelve thousand blocks and counting for their regular customers. They always cut more than they expected to sell. Their family motto was: "You can't sell what you don't have." A warm September and October meant extra income that would come in handy to buy new farm machinery.

Delivering ice in the summer was an enjoyable job for the men. They would take a hammer, break off the corner of a block, and throw it to any kid who was close by. This was a cool treat on a hot day.

Pond ice had to be between ten and twelve inches thick before it was cut. The thickness of the ice determined the height of the block, and saws determined the width and length. Kitchen ice boxes came in two sizes and blocks were cut to fit into either of these cavities. Small chunks could always be accommodated in larger ice boxes, but it was a bit of a chipping problem and also a waste to cut down a larger block.

In January and February, when ice became thick enough to cut into blocks, the work of filling the ice house would begin. Each block was put in place with a slight gap from the other blocks, making it look like a tile floor with a thick grout line. A large corn broom was used to fill the cracks with sawdust. Next, each layer of ice blocks was covered with an inch of sawdust. Ice layers would eventually reach the top of the barn and an ice stairway was filled in as men worked their way out of the barn.

Reg remembered his dad saying, "One year, we did not fill the cracks properly and many blocks welded themselves to adjoining blocks. We smashed a lot of blocks trying to pry them apart."

Reg supervised the loading of the ice house and, when he was not there, Silvia, his oldest daughter was in charge. Getting the ice out was just as important as packing it in correctly. Chutes were built in along each wall of the ice houses so the shovelling of sawdust outside did not take long. Large piles of sawdust outside meant that summer was nearing an end and business had been good.

The Norwood Mill Pond was one source of good ice. Before chain saws and round gas-driven circular saws, large handsaws, made specifically for sawing ice, were used. First, long straight lines were sawn along the ice and then cross lines formed square blocks. Men watched for weeds coming up on their saw cuts. If the colour green popped up, they stopped sawing as blocks of ice with weeds inside were not welcomed by their customers. Once the blocks were cut, men used tongs to grip each block. Each ice block was pushed down into the water as far as possible, and, as it bobbed back up, it was quickly pulled onto the surface of the ice. A good bit of water splashed up as each ice block bounced up, making the men's working surface slippery and dangerous.

Blocks were then slid across the ice to a waiting wagon or truck bed. There, two other men would pick up the blocks, place them onto a wagon or truck bed, and haul them to the ice house. Horses were used to pull the wagons and many families used hay fork equipment to move ice blocks from holes to wagons and trucks. Horses were shod with the newest shoes farmers could get. Sharp shoes kept working horses from slipping and going down into freezing water.

Sawdust was brought in from sawmills in summer or late fall, and a tarp covered the pile to keep the fall rains and snow from freezing it solid. Filling ice houses was not a one-man job and families got together and pooled their equipment and manpower to make the job easier. Walking on the ice around an open hole was a slippery adventure. Anyone losing his footing would have to be pulled out of the freezing water.

When his long-time customers started buying electric refrigerators, Reg knew that these families would not be buying ice for the next summer. Soon all of his customers would be gone. What would he do when ice blocks were no longer needed? Ironically, chain saws without bar oil, conveyors that could move the blocks from the water to the truck, studded truck tires, electric winches, and sawdust augers, were making cutting, hauling, and storing ice much easier for him. The only problem was that refrigeration would kill the old-time ice business.

Reg knew that he could continue cutting ice and storing blocks in his ice houses until his customers on the lakes got electricity and refrigeration. His ice business would become smaller and smaller each year, but he also knew customers would need to buy refrigerators that were trucked in and installed. Opening up a small store and stocking refrigerators and other home appliances would be easy and profitable, if he could get the appliances to sell.

After World War II there was a shortage in most consumer products and whatever was produced, no matter what the colour, style, or quality, would sell to a waiting public. Reg opened up his store and did very well supplying his customers with new appliances. Reg did have to pull a few strings to get these appliances to sell to his customers. This is when knowing the local Member of Parliament and having a lodge membership paid off.

Many cottagers on the Lakes north of Norwood; Stony Lake, White, Caush, Clear, Round, Belmont, and others would still need ice as the islands and remote shorelines did not have electricity. Reg's Cousin Ed was still cutting ice on Pigeon Lake for the big house. Sir Edward Kempt owned Sandy Point and his house not only had ice boxes but it was the only home in the area with ice-powered air conditioning. In the middle of the house, a steel silo went from the ground floor to the second floor. It was kept full of ice all summer and the air passing around this silo kept the house cool. However, Sir Edward would soon have his own electric generating station built on the point and would no longer need ice.

Reg and Gloria decided that Reg needed a day off to sit and think. They had exhausted the topic many times and could not see a future for their children. They would be the first generation not to have a portion of their income from cutting and storing ice. Time to think would mean a walk in the woods. Reg asked Silvia, his oldest daughter, if she would take a walk with him in the back fifty. Silvia was a senior at high school and was weighing her options. University was not a consideration and at this time the college system was not in place.

Silvia, knowing her dad, said, "Sure, when do you want to go"?

"Let's take a walk Saturday morning." Taking Saturday off and not working at real things, but just talking and planning was a big step for Reg. The conversation with Silvia was not about how to stay in the ice cutting business but how do we serve this new customer. The short walk turned into a long walk. The discussion turned into a meal time dialogue. All their neighbours had the same problem, change, but change came at them in different ways. Their friends and neighbours in Norwood grew up on family farms that all had a dual purpose: to produce cattle for milk and also for good meat. On their one-hundred acre or two-hundred acre farms, farmers would also have a hen house with fifty or sixty laying chickens, a pig pen with two or three sows that would litter about eight or twelve piglets every year, and draft horses that could be bred. Some farmers had a few sheep and the odd one would have a small herd of goats. Ducks and geese were also common. Family farms were very successful before mechanization, as two-hundred acres with ten to twenty acres of wetland and bush could sustain a family nicely and also provide cash income from selling eggs, butter, maple syrup, fire wood, and extra quarters of meat. Work was hard, taxes were low, and costs were minimal. This would all change rapidly.

Small carriage-style horses were phased out as the automobile and half-ton truck replaced them. Ploughed winter roads meant that most places were accessible by car.

Small family farming was very efficient at producing food and income, but the writing was on the wall. Each year the price received for goods was not enough to keep up with the cost to produce them. Farmers had to produce more for less, year after year, if they wanted to stay in business. The only way to produce more for less was to specialize, mechanize, squeeze costs, and get larger. When mechanization came on-stream, change accelerated, leaving timid and small producers behind. Change dictated that quantity was more important than quality, and could it travel to market and sit on a shelf?

In the early fifties, tractors were introduced. For the small sum of one thousand dollars or less, farmers could buy a machine with horsepower and pulling power that was much superior to that of the draft horses being fed and looked after in their barns. Harnesses had to be maintained. Horses needed daily exercise, and hooves needed to be shod every so many months. Horse-drawn equipment had a long tongue that ran up between a team of horses. As the team pulled a machine, its moving wheels turned a belt that in turn powered the mower, rake or binder or whatever machinery was attached. New tractors had a three-point hitch on the back, so a long tongue was no longer needed.

Switching to a tractor for power was a big step. Horse-pulled equipment had to be changed to machinery that a tractor could pull, or to equipment that hooked onto the tractor and ran off the power takeoff. Driven by the clutch, the power takeoff or PTO was a shaft which extended out of the rear of the tractor. This shaft powered whatever equipment was being pulled, so that the tractor engine drove the bailer or mower or whatever machine was being pulled. Later on, hydraulic hoses further changed options on equipment.

Early PTOs were not covered in protective shielding. Loose pants, shirts, or belts could get caught and wrapped up when a farmer least expected it to happen. Arms and legs were broken, hands were mangled, and sometimes complete bodies were spun around a live PTO.

One day, Reg's neighbour was showing some city relatives his new tractor and hay bailer. At the same moment that he motioned his son to engage the PTO, a breeze blew open the front panel of his Sunday jacket and it caught on the revolving shaft. He instinctively bent over to free it. In a second his tie caught and the shaft pulled him in head first. It was all over in the blink of an eye.

Tragically, in the previous year, Reg's brother, skidding out a pine tree with their mare, was also killed in an accident. The tree was being dragged out butt first as it had fallen into the woods in such a way that the top was not handy and it was difficult to swing in his mare to hook up the top. On the way out to the landing, the tree caught around a small stump. The whip action of the tree top flicked a two-foot section of a branch into the air. It caught Reg's brother in the back of the head and broke his neck. He was dead before he hit the ground.

Those farmers, who did not figure out that they had to produce more for less, often had to take part-time jobs to provide enough income for their families to keep living on farms. Sometimes these part-time farmers worked for years before they realized that they were working two jobs for no returns. Growing larger and becoming more efficient were the keys to staying in business. They had to specialize in eggs, meat chickens, milk, beef, sheep, or goats. Staying in mixed farming meant poverty. When asked what he would do if he won the Irish sweepstakes, one old timer quipped, "I'd just keep farming until the money is all gone."

Reg saw the inevitable movement to mechanization and realized that as soon as he had tools to cut and store ice more efficiently, that ice would no longer be needed. Imagine a chain saw cutting the ice, a conveyor moving the blocks to a truck, a lift to move the ice into the ice house, and a blower putting sawdust around the blocks. The problem was that customers no longer needed the ice blocks at any price. His family's encyclopaedic knowledge of cutting, handling, and storing ice would all soon be forgotten.

What to do with all the horses? Farm tractors were taking over the role of the draft horses. Once farm machinery was converted to being shaft-driven by tractors, or new machinery was purchased to go on a tractor's three-point hitch, horses were only used to skid logs or pull wagons. However, for that odd time that horses were needed to pull a tractor out of mud or snow, a farmer often felt justified in keeping his favourite team.

Percheron, Belgian, Clydesdale, and mixed breeds were the common work horses in the Norwood farm community. Every farm had a minimum of one team. Most had four or five horses, a mare in foal, and a young team that was being groomed to take over as older horses were put out to pasture. Somehow farmers would have to reluctantly make the tough decision to get rid of their horses.

The Norwood town dump was on the east side of the eighth line of Asphodel, south of Number Seven Highway. One day on a trip to the town dump, Reg and his dad Reginald stopped at the field where the horses were being fenced in before slaughter. The slaughterhouse for horses was on the west side of the same gravel road. Both men noticed that there was plenty of water available but no feed. The field had been tramped flat and hard by the thousands of horses before the ones waiting that day.

"Reg, there must be a least two hundred horses in this field. Just a few years ago, I could not afford most of these teams in here today. It's like watching your life pass by." Tears trickled down the old man's cheeks and his voice could not speak anymore. The two men just stood and watched all these beautiful horses.

Thousands of horses per year were turned into dog food. The slaughterhouse operated for over ten years until all of the surplus horses were gone. Like farming, there was little money in the dog food business, as slaughterhouses all over the continent were supplying the same small market. It is interesting to note that beef prices were also depressed during this time.

The same loyalty that farmers developed over the years to their horses soon switched to a tractor manufacturer. Companies that recognized this remained in business. Farmers are still referred to as having green blood, green for John Deere and red for Massey Harris.

Silvia was not interested nor could the family afford sending Silvia to university. She would like to make her living by farming. She always enjoyed being around chickens and decided to raise chickens for meat. At the time, there were no contracts and farmers took their chances on being able to sell what they produced. The risk of boom and bust disappeared when corporations began to write contracts with farmers to raise chickens.

The deal with farmers was very simple. The farmers would build chicken barns. The corporation would give them small chicks and food to produce hens. Farmers would be paid so many cents per pound for live chickens at the end of an eight to ten-week life cycle. Keeping chickens alive meant money in the bank. Corporations contracted farmers to turn over their live inventory between four and five times a year.

The heat in the summer and cold in the winter had to be managed to keep the death toll down. Disease, mould, and wild predators had to be eliminated. Restricting access to people, other than those working in a barn, was very important too. High school students, who were often hired to do the job of catching chickens, would be allowed to work for only one producer. Their names would be circulated to the other chicken houses. Since boots or clothing could transfer bacteria and diseases from one barn to the other, movement between two barns was forbidden.

Silvia took a chance and signed on with a new buyer who was opening restaurants specializing in chicken dishes. When the owners of these Chicken Chalet Restaurants were blocked by the Federal government's Wage and Price controls, they could not increase the price of their meals. To stay in business, senior management decided that the only thing they could do was decrease the cost of supply. They invested in a plan to produce quality chickens at the lowest cost by signing contracts with private farmers. Management would provide feed for the chicks and then would specify the weight of the chickens they required. This would guarantee a bird to meet their needs. Silvia signed on and was soon producing the quality bird specified. Inadvertently, management found a huge market, business boomed, and more chickens were needed. Silvia's chicken houses grew larger and larger and soon three new, three-storey houses were in full production. Each floor held fifty-thousand chickens. A floor a week were being caught and shipped.

Each year she had to produce more for less. This was also on the minds of other farmers who wanted to stay in business. Consumers wanted fruit, meat, and vegetables at the lowest price possible. The old idea of growing vegetables and fruits for taste and nutritional value was no longer on the horizon.

One day, Silvia noticed that the chicken manure piled up in a field close to the barn was being devoured by beef cows. They were eating chicken manure like it was silage from the corn silo. Silvia, like her dad, was a Result Merchant: "Let's see what happens if the cows continue to eat this stuff."

Sure enough, after a summer of eating chicken manure, the cows gained more weight than if they had been on pasture all summer. Silvia could save in two ways: the time needed to spread manure on fields, and acres of pasture could be replaced by a steady supply of manure. She could reduce her costs of producing both chickens and beef. Staying in business and earning enough to keep her head above water was important. Other neighbours observed what was happening and started to copy this diet for their cattle. Chicken manure became a sought-after cattle food source. Since most farmers did not kill their own cattle, these animals were shipped to large slaughterhouses.

The chicken-manure-feeding practice spread until Ontario's Department of Agriculture heard about it. Instantly, the cheap food supply was banned. Only the local tomatoe growers were happy, as they got their best fertilizer back.

As Silvia said, "The government thinks chicken-shit tomatoes are okay and chicken-shit beef is bad. That provincial government knows a lot about shit."

Jack, the youngest in Reg's family, was very inquisitive. Like his mom, he was always questioning why things were done in a certain way. Jack enjoyed school and excelled in subjects that asked "what if" questions. Memorizing facts and repeating them was not interesting, but he did understand that some basics in arithmetic, English and science had to be memorized.

He often saw ways to improve and speed up a process. For example, Jack watched as the men pushed ice blocks down into the water and then floated them up onto the ice surface. He asked why they did this and discovered that the weight of the ice block was too much for one person to lift up onto the ice hour after hour. Jack recognized it as the same technique needed to pull up an anchor or a heavy net of fish on the side of a dory bobbing in the waves.

Jack was young and he had only his experience and his family's accumulated knowledge about ice. As blocks were removed from the ice house, he would ask his dad if he could experiment with different types of coverings, boxes, and shields to see what happened as ice melted. As the ice business declined each year, Jack had more and more blocks with which to experiment. He was sure that it was the sun's rays, and not the air temperature, that caused ice to melt. He thought that the sun's rays 'cooked' the ice.

His grade eleven science teacher, Steven Etchels, was a person with a huge intellect and a questioning mind. Mr. Etchels challenged his students, taking time to understand individual students and to find out what captivated them. When his student, Jack, had to write an essay, the topic to interest him would probably have to do with ice, the family business. Mr. Etchels clearly stated for each available science topic you could take any position, agree or disagree, but you could not sit on the fence. Sitting on the fence was a mug wug, your mug on one side and the wug on the other. There was no correct answer to the topic. Each student was evaluated by ideas and writing ability. Jack put his name on the essay list next to the topic: *The sun, not air temperature, melts ice.* He was on his way.

Much later in life, Jack Wilson proved to himself that global warming was an equivocation to be used creatively by the science community as a means for their own ends.

The hypothesis of Jack's essay was that, although temperature is important, it's the direct rays of the sun that causes ice to melt. For his experiments, Jack put different materials like cardboard, black plastic, sawdust, and dirt on the ice on his family's farm pond. Then he put the same cardboard, black plastic and other materials a few inches above the ice and watched as the ice melted. Jack concluded that temperature does melt ice, but it is the direct rays of the sun that penetrate ice, make ice crystallize, and then make ice fall apart.

Jack's curiosity made him question if polar ice was melting. Maybe polar ice was melting and disappearing, not because of global warming and rising temperatures, but because of the changes in the amount and intensity of sunlight that polar regions were receiving. A few degrees up or down might not have an impact on ice conditions, but hours of sunlight and the direct rays of sunlight likely would affect other things like plant growth, weather patterns, and the amount of skin cancer in humans, if bare skin is exposed to the rays of the sun.

Jack's hypothesis, as a grade eleven science student, was that the receeding polar ice was due to the sun's intensity and not because of temperature change. He thought that scientists were probably using global warming for their own interests and not because they had researched the real cause, changes in the direct rays of the sun.

Jack called it the "Ice Box Theory". He knew that ice at the top of an ice box kept things below cool. When the ice was gone, the box warmed up and all the stored food spoiled.

Jack speculated that the sun's rays percolating through ice are responsible for breaking up the thick ice of the polar regions. Once the protective ice cap is destroyed, black water and exposed rocks absorb even more heat from the sun's rays. When the polar ice caps and glaciers around the world are reduced, the ice box below warms up. In short, the sun's rays have changed and it is those rays that are destroying the ice. Once the ice is gone, the world will warm up.

The only reason Jack did not get an A+ on his paper was his comment on the speculation that the science community was using rising world temperatures to scare an uneducated population into allocating funds for pet projects. Speculation was not allowed in Mr Etchel's research essays. Students were graded down when they veered away from facts. "Let the reader draw his own conclusions."

Jack was happy to get feedback on his work. Mr. Etchel wrote a comment on the bottom of his paper. "A. You might be right or wrong; the important part is that you are thinking. Congratulations!"

It was years later, after Jack had been in his arena ice business for a while, that he also discovered a solution for the melting of the polar ice and those ice-filled, frozen rivers called glaciers.

Jack followed his family's ice business in a different way. He loved to skate and fortunately lived close to the Norwood Skating Rink on Spring Street. If it had not been torn down, it would still sit at 36 Spring Street, nestled in a slight ravine, a site especially chosen for its natural ice. The rink's steel-roofed building had bleachers at the south end and two dressing rooms down the west side, one for the home team and one for the visiting team. Each room had its own woodstove. Tucked into the southwest corner was a snack bar. In the southeast corner was the boiler room. Lou High was the rink manager, responsible for making the ice, putting lines onto the ice, cleaning the dressing rooms, and managing the complete facility. The only help she had was from volunteer kids. Being one of the "Rink Rats" was a prized job for any kid strong enough to shovel snow and push a four-foot ice scraper. Jack loved his status as a Rink Rat and he hoped to move up to Head Rink Rat when he got older and stronger.

Every late fall, Jack and Lou took garden rakes and smoothed out the arena sand. Then they packed it down with a heavy cement roller. In early November they started to flood the rink. Putting a light spray on the sand and then building up coats of ice was an art. Since local weather reports were often innaccurate, Lou went with what she thought the temperature would be.

The flooding hose, rolled up on the floor in the boiler room, was fed out of a small opening that had a roller on the bottom and sides. Lou took the end of the hose with the nozzle, and as she pulled the hose to the end of the rink, Jack would guide the hose out of the opening. Once the hose was completely pulled out, Jack turned on a large valve, and Lou started flooding. She came backwards towards the south end, sweeping the surface from left to right, as Jack slowly pulled the hose back into the boiler room. It took fifteen or twenty minutes to flood the entire rink. On cold days and nights they put on a flood every thirty minutes.

Jack loved his job, especially when Lou said, "Put on your skates", and let Jack skate the wet ice between flooding. He was in a full-sized indoor arena by himself with a stick and puck.

Once the ice had been flooded a number of times, building up two or three inches, it was time to put on the hockey lines. After painting on the blue lines, centre red line, goalie lines, and then five circles and nine red dots, Jack was ready to sit beside the warm boiler-room stove. He became Lou's third hand and learned how to use string and tape to make straight lines and circles of any size needed.

As the winter progressed and the ice built up, the step up into the player's box and into other doors leading onto the ice decreased from twelve inches to eight and then six inches. After every build-up of an inch or so of ice, new lines were painted over the old faded lines.

Jack loved art and doodling and often thought it would be fun to paint drawings on ice. He knew that the curling rink crew also had to build ice and paint circles and lines required to meet curling standards.

Not everyone could paint on ice. Jack decided that this would be a good job to earn some extra spending money. Practising on ice blocks at home, he found different paints and other materials that worked well to colour ice. Painting on a huge surface and blending colours seemed to come naturally to him. He even found that he could make ice whiter in colour, and that no milk farmer would ever give away this trade secret.

Curling rinks were a special challenge as curling lanes had to be level. A lane that sloped in one direction or another was a disaster. Jack worked on a technique to flood and build even, smooth, and level ice on both a small four-lane rink or on a large twelve-lane rink. After each game of curling, the ice was sprayed with a fine hose, much like one used to spray weeds. The ice pebbles that formed from careful spraying allowed the stones to curl.

When a granite rock rides on top of the ice pebbles, its weight melts the top of the pebbles. The water formed allows the stone to slide more easily down the ice. This is similar to the film of water created by skates as skaters move down the ice. As the game continues in curling, ice pebbles wear down and flatten and the stone begins to curl differently, depending on the temperature of the ice surface. After sprayings between games, the pebbles eventually have to be scraped off the surface and the process starts all over again.

Jack became an expert not only at putting down pebbles, but also at experimenting with different types of water. He found that aerated or softened water, or water that had certain minerals added to it would affect the speed of a curling stone. He began trying similar experiments on skating rinks.

The growth of televised hockey and curling demanded whiter ice and sharper lines for the cameras. When lacrosse did not follow his colour suggestions, television cameras could not pick up the ball, and viewers of that sport turned off their televisions.

Jack's painting and ice-making business expanded to two and then three employees. Sara was his first employee. This part-time position quickly turned into a full-time career.

After the first winter with an employee, Jack realized that he also needed a warehouse.

"Sara, how would you like to help me build a warehouse this summer?"

"I guess so. Not sure how to help, but I will learn."

Sara was off the farm and the eldest of the pack. Her farming parents had five girls and no boys. Age, not gender, determined who was on a farm work crew. Sara helped her dad build every shed, stall and lean-to on the farm.

Jack's new building was positioned on a lot in such a way that would allow future additions, if they were required. Inside, small experimental ice surfaces, four-feet by four-feet and at table-top height, took up most of the floor space. Refrigerators and freezers were cannibalized and with the stainless steel grills pulled out of family restaurants, that were going out of business, small ice rinks were Jerry rigged to do the job. Jack continued to experiment by changing components in the water and by using different dyes and paints.

Some arenas were moving to plastic lines and logos, but the risk of cutting through or chipping creative designs limited these customers to small, low-cost projects.

Advertising on the ice surface drove Jack's business to become bigger and bigger. He trained his staff well. He loved to be in the warehouse experimenting.

His well-paid crew was called Rink Rat Artists. He and these artists found themselves booked year-round in major centre arenas around North America. They were responsible not only for the ice in these rinks, but also for the lines and graphics for special occasions. Celebrations, Olympics, you name it and Jack's crew would be on that ice. Jack also supplied the special waters that he had formulated to make ice harder or softer at certain temperatures. Ice for hockey players was not ice that was suitable for figure skating. Jack took a few bookings in Europe, before he realized that the cost of flying and getting products overseas put him at a cost disadvantage for regular run-of-the-mill jobs at home. For these jobs in Europe, he would only go when something special or technically-difficult was required.

One technique that Jack mastered was the art of burying paint that would only glow when black light shone on the design. The first time he experimented with this technique was at Maple Leaf Gardens in Toronto, where he knew the manager well. He had a plan to paint the ice after the third coat, so that it would be buried under the layers above. The letters spelled out "GO LEAFS GO" and they covered the complete surface of the arena. The thinking was, once the Leafs scored, the regular lights would be dimmed, the black lights would turn on, and the ice would light up. The only problem with this new idea was that the Leafs had to score a goal. Jack was a true and blue Leaf's fan and he suffered with all of us, year after year, all the excuses...

One day, while he was trying new water and a new thickness, he happened to have the freezing tray next to a large window that was always kept open for light, but not for direct sunshine. Eureka. He stumbled over the solution for stopping the sun's rays from melting ice.

He formulated his new product and could hardly wait to try it out. His first large test was conducted on an Ontario country side road. On the way to his family's cottage, there was a completely flat stretch of road with no surrounding trees, just open corn fields. Jack worked on his own free time and used his own money. He was not yet familiar with how to access government grants for this type of research work.

Snow banks on the north side of this country road faced south. Those northern banks melted first in the spring. He decided to apply his new product on both snow banks in fifty-foot intervals and wait until spring to see if the snow and ice would last longer on the test strips. Sure enough, when March and then April's sun's rays started percolating through the snow, the snow banks with the test strips remained intact two weeks longer. Jack knew that he was on the right track.

Jack's new product was made from waste, it was in abundance and it worked. Heated up and flaked, this product became white, reflecting almost one hundred percent of the sun's rays. Next, Jack found a way to produce it cheaply and in a form that could be mixed with water, so it could be sprayed. The first trials of his new solution were done at ski resorts on the side hills, which melted too early in the spring. Every winter snow-making crews spent extra time and money building up these trouble spots, so more runs could remain open for March Break skiers. If Jack's solution worked, resorts could be open longer and could make more money.

Other customers for his new product were big trucking firms eager to extend the length of their hauling season to northern communities. The most cost-efficient supply line in the north was trucking, and this meant trucking over winter ice highways to get supplies into northern warehouses. Once connecting lakes were frozen and prepared for the trucking season, ice highways were busy. Extending the season by two weeks would be a dream come true. One oil and exporting company sprayed Jack's compound one-hundred feet on each side of an ice highway, allowing the ice to remain solid and able to withstand daily truck traffic north and south for two extra weeks. These extra weeks in a short season saved the high costs of tonnage that was formerly flown in.

Jack speculated that if his compound was sprayed by airplane onto the Arctic ice shelf, the polar ice would not shrink.

Jack had first come up with his famous "Ice Box Theory" in high school. His theory explained why the polar ice caps were disappearing and the world was warming up. His high school education ended at grade twelve, because he did not go back for grade thirteen. So, Jack's theory was very simple. He did not have the formal education to make anything complicated or difficult to understand. He saw the globe warming up as a simple logical problem with simple logical causes. Now, he had stumbled onto a solution for slowing down the earth's gradual increases in temperature and a way to cool off the world. Jack's thinking was out of the box. He thought big.

He did not have a soap box to stand on or a scientific journal to submit articles to, but he was the expert on making and painting ice and on changing the properties of ice to suit any situation.

His original "Ice Box Theory" was based on his experiences as a young man helping his dad cut ice to fill all those customers' ice boxes. He compared the world's ice caps at the North and South Poles to the ice in the top of the ice box. Winds blow over both masses of ice. In the northern hemisphere, these cold winds come south and keep us cooler than if there was no ice for the winds to blow over. When the ice reduces in size or starts to disappear, the winds have less cold mass to blow over and the land south of the ice cap will warm up.

In the southern hemisphere, the Antarctic ice cap works in the same way and keeps that end of the world cool.

"The key," Jack explained, to anyone that would take the time to listen, "is to understand how ice melts, something most people do not understand. Heat and the sun's radiation melt ice. The main reason for the polar ice melting is the sun's rays and not the air temperature."

Jack demonstrated by placing an ice cube into a microwave oven and melting it. Since the air temperature inside the oven didn't change, it demonstrated that wasn't what melted the ice cube, microwaves did. The higher the setting the faster the ice melted. He also pointed out that every spring the sun, not warm air, melted winter snow and ice.

As a boy, Jack lived in Norwood and had a paper route that started out east on Highway #7 towards Havelock, where it swung south on Mill Street through the railroad subway to the last house. He walked by both ponds in Norwood and he watched the Mill Pond and Upper Pond carefully, so he would know when the ice on the Upper Pond was safe to cross. He put his skates on at the east end and skated the length of the pond to the small dam. Not only did he save time delivering his papers this way, but he had a lot of fun along the way.

Every spring he watched the ice go out. This event ended his short cut for that winter and he had to walk along the highway again and not skate or ride his bike across the pond. As a kid, Jack could balance a paper-route bag over his shoulder while riding his bike on glare ice. Speed helped keep things straight.

As winter ended annually, Jack noticed that the sun seemed to cook the ice. Even on cool days, the March sun did its work. On days that were cloudy and warm, the ice did not melt very much. A week of cloudy warm weather did not soften the ice enough to make it unsafe for him to short cut it across to the dam.

Long before Jack, early settlers discovered that any ice and snow under the layer of sawdust, where they were cutting wood and clearing land, took a long time to melt. That was how they learned to use sawdust to pack ice houses. Sawdust was a good insulator and they could keep ice from melting quickly. Covering ice with just about any sun-blocking material makes it last longer than ice exposed to the direct rays of the sun.

The concept that it was the sun's rays that melted ice and snow was hard to grasp for many of Jack's friends.

Jack told them, "When ice melts it gives off coolness. But when the sun's rays penetrate and destroy the ice, the air temperature is not cooled. If ice melts from warm moving air, the air is cooled. The sun is like a giant microwave oven. It cooks the ice but no coolness is generated. When polar ice is destroyed by the sun, there is no ice left to cool the passing air."

On the family farm in Norwood Jack was amazed to see his dad out ploughing a field first thing in the spring. Next to it in the sugar bush his uncle would still be on frozen ground collecting the very last of the sap. The trees, mainly maple, with some spruce mixed in, blocked the sun from penetrating to the ground.

"Take an ice box out into the backyard, take off its top, and expose the ice to the sun. The ice will be destroyed very quickly and the food down below will not be any cooler than if the top was left on. The rapid decrease and disappearance in ice, because of the sun's rays, means the food below will now heat up."

What causes the world to heat up? Jack had opinions on that as well. He said, "There are only three sources of heat: the sun, the earth's core, and nuclear power."

"The sun and its stored products like petroleum, peat bogs, natural gas, coal and wood can be turned into useable products or processed into fuel. Wind and rain are directly generated by the sun's heating of the land and waters. Vegetation, fish and animals of all kinds rely on photosynthesis. At one time, our planet Earth was blue water, green vegetation, and brown deserts, with two white ice caps. When man came along, he paved millions of square miles of land, over a period of time roofed millions of buildings, stripped forests, and polluted the large oceans."

"The sun, beating on black asphalt in the summer, causes roads to heat up. When pilots in small aircraft cross a wide highway, an updraft will lift their planes. Flying across a forest or green field of corn and then hitting the updraft over a highway is always a thrill. These updrafts are used by raptors or hawks to soar around the sides of a highway or high above, getting a free ride back up to their lofty hunting positions."

"The three levels of government are the largest land owners in the country. They own the streets, road, and highways and are the largest landlord of buildings."

Jack was not short of opinions. He could criticise the Pope about how he conducted mass. When asked about air pollution, and how carbon monoxide and smog are causing global warming, he just nodded. He would tell them about his cousin Allen.

Allen was born and raised in downtown London, England. He was born before the Second World War and lived through the turmoil. After the war, both of his parents worked hard to rebuild their lives and their home. Each Saturday, Allen was allowed to go to the local movie house. Allen had no brothers or sisters so he would go by himself. In the mid-to-late fifties, most homes and small businesses were heated with coal-burning fireplaces. Diesel oil, burned by buses, trucks, and some autos, was often of low quality. Consequently, the air quality in general was very poor and just breathing was a struggle. Blowing your nose would fill your hanky with black soot.

One of the reasons Allen was allowed to go to the movie house by himself was that it was on the same block as their walk-up, and he could reach out and touch the walls of the buildings all the way to the movie house. Sometimes the air was so black that he could get lost walking down his street, and in the movie theatre he had to sit in the front half to be able to see the screen clearly.

Londoners, who are in their late sixties and seventies, will verify the extreme level of pollution in London during those days. Cold and damp, England was not a very pleasant place to be. In fact, it would be much like living in China today. Those who have never seen clean air do not know what they are missing. Finally, laws were put in place and enforced. Coal-burning fireplaces were outlawed, diesel fuel was cleaned up, and industries could no longer push their waste products up the stack. Today, air in England is much cleaner and smog and soot have been drastically reduced. You can even blow your nose at the end of the day and not fill a tissue with black guck.

Then Jack would pause and say, "When England had a century of industrial pollution floating in the air, the weather was cool, damp, cold, and rainy. We have cleaned up much of our old ways and as a result we now have many sunny days and it is a lot warmer."

Jack was a keen observer of many things. He reasoned that the sunlight hitting the moon bounces directly to earth. On a clear night, with a full moon, it is almost bright enough outside to read a newspaper, but moonlight is not warm. Jack did not understand how the sun's rays bouncing off the CO^2 in the atmosphere could heat up the earth. Airplanes are darn cold when they fly a few thousand feet above the earth.

One of Jack's friends, Greg, was a pro bass fisherman who struggled each year with sunburns. Pro-fishermen are on the water as much as possible, and they wear long-sleeved protective shirts, pants, hats, sunglasses, and sometimes scarves around their necks to reduce the effects of the sun bouncing off the water. Greg was nicknamed 'the racoon' at the end of one fishing season when his eyes, protected by the sunglasses, were like a racoon's in their white colouration.

In the spring, when the sun shines, lake ice directly above any rock shoals or above stumps just under the surface of the ice melts first. The sun penetrates through the ice, heating up the objects below first. Then warmer water around the rocks and stumps melts the ice above. Jack reasoned that the thick ice in the polar regions must be penetrated by the sun in the same way, heating the rocks or sea water below. Also, mountain glaciers slide down a mountain side on a film of water created by friction and by the sun's rays. These penetrating rays through the polar ice allow plant and animal organisms to grow in the cold arctic regions and provide food and nourishment for larger water life. The sun is doing much more than just bouncing off the thick, white, polar ice caps.

Jack, in his modest non-judgemental way, would point out to whoever would listen to him that the science community is using Global Warming as a tool to catch the public's attention. The science community wants the public to react and put pressure on governments to reduce the levels of pollution in the air, water, and land we live on. Governments do not lead. They follow. In Jack's opinion using a public opinion poll to determine policy is called playing it safe or following the herd. No politician wants to be the lead cow wearing the bell. Our free press would quickly lead that politician to the slaughterhouse.

Jack said the science community did not really understand what was causing global warming; they were just using it as a tool to correct other problems that needed to be addressed.

Jack knew that he did not have the qualifications of a learned scholar, so he would not have the support of people who could make the required changes. To initiate change, people relied on experts for opinions and recommendations. Jack had no letters behind his name. He only had forty years of making ice.

Jack also had his own theory on temperatures.

Again, Jack would tell anyone that would listen. His employees often became his audience. "Assume for one minute that the average daily temperature has increased by one whole degree. The way I think is that every day of the year on average it is one degree warmer. If you are in the Artic in the winter and it is normally minus 42 degrees so it would now be minus 41 that day. It still feels cold and not much is melting. In the fall and spring instead of the temperature being minus 5 it is minus 4. It is still cool and nothing is melting. Jack liked to say don't get ahead of me please. So in the summer if the temperature during the day normally gets to plus 10 Celsius it now is plus 11. The number of frost free days increase. Is the science community telling the world that one degree increase a few days in the summer can melt all that polar ice that quickly?

Today's scientists have the wrong dog barking up the wrong tree. I have been in the ice business too long. I think they have the data in the wrong order. When the sun melts the ice, the world heats up. When the sun is blocked the world cools down. Changes in temperature are a **result not a cause**. Nice try guys. I am moving to Missouri on this one."

Jack's favourite expression was visible throughout his company's physical plant. "I am walking backwards, when you walk backwards you stand up taller and you can see further."

"Today, scientists say, "Burning fossil fuels is generating carbon dioxide. Increasing the carbon dioxide creates a green house effect.

Warming up melts the polar ice caps and glaciers. This is Bass akwards."

In Jack's way of thinking the reduction in ice warms up the planet. The burning of fossil fuels and the build up of carbon dioxide is definitely a problem and should be addressed but Jack warned not to incorrectly link it to global warming. Find out why the ice is melting. Stop burning fossil fuels is an important issue and should be addressed and stopped. "If you go back and look at the data for previous ice ages what came first?"

"Get this, the world is locked in an ice age and the thick sheets of ice are miles high extending across Canada and well down into the United States. Then suddenly someone starts up a gas guzzling, diesel stinking, smoke belching machine which results in a cloud of carbon dioxide which forms a greenhouse effect and the ice melts. No, the Icebox Theory is that the sun melts the ice. When you have less ice to cool the winds, the planet heats up. Jack was humble in his ability to show the opposite. He would often muse with his friends by saying, "I haven't quite worked out how we are going to go south and bring all our topsoil back that was scraped away by the advancing sheets of ice."

A cellular phone rang. Jack picked it up immediately. Business came first. The Manager of the Cow Palace in Warkworth, Ontario was calling to have the arena ice painted for the opening celebration of fall hockey.

The old Cow Palace no longer existed. The first arena in Warkworth was an old cow barn used for the local fair, housing cattle that were going to be shown in the ring. The name stuck and everyone continued to refer to the new arena as the Cow Palace too. You guessed it. This year the arena committee wanted Jack to appropriately paint a herd of cows at centre ice, Holstein and Guernsey cows grazing on the local hills. This was in honour of the Roe family who had operated the Warkworth Cheese factory for years. It now sat empty.

Jack never delegated this assignment to his five Rink Rat Artists. He cherished taking the truck from Richmond Hill down through Norwood and Hastings on his way to Warkworth. After the job was done, he always found an excuse to go towards Campbellford to stop at the Empire Cheese Factory Store so he could load up on fresh cheddar cheese curd and on old cheddar cheese. Jack would eat a pound of squeaky curd on the way home and reminisce about his years growing up, when he had four uncles who made cheddar cheese. After the Ontario Milk Marketing Board and the Ontario government put rules and regulations in place, smaller cheddar cheese makers across the province were driven out. The Warkworth cheese factory was just one of the hundreds of small factories that went out of business. But that is another story.

Sometimes Jack chose not to listen to instructions and this was one of those occasions. He was alone with the rink manager in Warkworth when he decided this. He had met the Roe family and he had a sixth sense about what would be appropriate for the occasion. Jack dropped on the ice at seven p.m. and started to sketch. Working on cold ice in warm clothing was fun, but after a couple of hours he needed a break to get re-heated and to get his fingers working. Jack warmed up in the Zamboni room, drank his hot tea, and headed back out onto the ice.

Jack painted an aging Jersey cow having her last calf. The scene was on mid ice. The elderly Jersey cow was turning sideways, looking at the newborn calf she had delivered. Off to one side was the family dog and downwind was a coyote waiting for the afterbirth. Coyotes move in and eat the sack and fluids from the birth and, if given an opportunity, take the newborn calf too. This wise old mother was a match for the coyote.

The big new Zamboni was pulled out and the flooding began. The ice shaving knives were pulled up and warm water was put down for the first two layers. The remaining floods used hot water to get a perfect, smooth-as-glass sheen. This ensured that the art work would not be cut up by the skaters. The images were in the ice for everyone to see.

Warkworth is a village of farm families and farm values and Jack took a chance that the local folk would see their life in an artistic expression. The Roe family sent Jack a letter that expressed it all.

Jack never had to worry about the renewal of his contract at the Cow Palace.

On the way home, Jack dropped into the Westwood Pit to tease Cal, as he did every chance he could, saying that he had forgotten to get the curd and block of old cheddar.

Just as Jack was about to get into his truck and head for Warkworth, he saw his son pulling into the parking lot. He was back from a work assignment in Arizona. Jack's son was nicknamed Chip by all the family, as he was a chip off the old block. His given name was Rambling, and he wore the name well. Chip was always requested back by any arena he was sent to in the USA as he teased the devil out of Americans and they loved it. He told his dad he really got the rink crew in Arizona. He stopped at one of the large grocery stores to pick up treats for the guys and was a little late getting to the arena. He told the arena crew that, coming from Canada, he was not used to the big US grocery stores and he got buried in the store. Once he had their attention, he told them he had taken a wrong turn down one of the snack aisles. As he was passing a large display of peanuts and chips, the display slid down and buried him. He was able to get his cell phone out of his pocket and, because he had just called the store and had the number in memory, he could dial the store for help. The rink crew were all ears and the bait was working.

The store reception called the in-store security guards and asked them to rush over and rescue the buried Canadian. I guess they heard the accent and assumed he was a Canadian. The store security guard headed for the fruit and vegetable section knowing that's where Canadians would be, but could not find the fresh produce section. Chip, as he was slowly stringing out the story, was unpacking two dozen donuts and a round of coffee. They knew they had been had once again.

The rink rats in Arizona were on guard since Chip had really taken them in the spring. When he arrived, he had a shoulder holster on his left shoulder. Pan-faced and saying nothing, he waited until someone asked him why he was wearing the shoulder strap. He looked down, then around and said, "At break, I will tell you what happened in Dallas, Texas." At coffee break in the boiler room, Chip took off the shoulder holster and drew the boys in.

Chip explained that as he headed for gate thirteen at the Dallas Airport, there was a line-up and he got into the pack. He did not realize that Homeland Security was implementing a new policy on weapon control. Realizing that taking all the weapons from passengers was a mistake, Homeland Security was trying a new system in Texas and Montana.

Under the new system, passengers were being trained on weapons use on airplanes, trains, busses, and all public commercial vehicles. Selected passengers, who had a gun licence, were given a special course on how to handle weapons on an airplane in a pressurized space environment. All volunteers were given a certificate which allowed them to carry weapons plus an HSC, a Homeland Security Card. Homeland security also gave them a twenty-five percent discount on flights. Chip reached in his pocket, and pulled out his wallet, opened it up, and placed it on the shovel handle just far enough that the men could not read the folded paper.

Chip went on to explain on his flight from Dallas, the stewardess announced, "Ladies and Gentleman, our Homeland security system wishes to welcome eight highly trained people on board. They are carrying weapons. Our special guest on this flight is Sheila Green, Silver Medal winner on our US Dart-throwing Olympic team. Sit back and enjoy your flight and rest assured that anyone wishing to hijack this aircraft will be looked after."

The arena manager taken in completely said, "Chip, I can't believe that Homeland Security is inching its way towards some common sense."

Chip turned, pulled out a huge marker from the shoulder holster and said, "Let's draw?" That's when the snowballs started.

Then Chip said to his dad, "Ironically you know, I had more problems getting the empty holster through customs than if it had been a loaded pistol. They stripped my luggage and just about had me dancing in my underwear. The only thing that saved me was a photo in my suitcase that showed me on the ice in the Gardens with a holster full of markers."

Jack and his son had a good laugh, then Jack climbed into the truck and he was on his way.

Epilogue

Well that concludes for now the stories of a small town in Ontario called Norwood. Remember how to find Norwood on Highway # 7. You just have to locate Centre Dummer and Rotten Lake and then drive a few miles south.

Thank you for taking the time to read these vignettes of life in Norwood.

For a glimpse of what is ahead....

Jack is working on finding a partner who has a lot of letters behind his name, so that he can get someone important to listen to his "ICE BOX THEORY" on global warming. After a full nights' sleep Jack awakened and realized his sun theory had a large flaw. Why did the sun not melt the ice at the South Pole like it did the North Pole? There is an answer!

Rose and Everett are hoping to find someone to help them get the public's attention on the windshield wiper disaster.

More stories are forthcoming. Until then, keep skating with your head up and your stick on the ice.

The last word is yours. If you have a book club, Rod has a story or just drop a line.

Rod@sawmillbooks.ca